School Friends

Secrets, hopes and dreams...
School friends are for ever!

Collect the whole **School Friends** series:

Party at Silver Spires
Dancer at Silver Spires
Dreams at Silver Spires

Magic at Silver Spires

Success at Silver Spires
Mystery at Silver Spires

...all featuring the Emerald dorm girls

First Term at Silver Spires
Drama at Silver Spires
Rivalry at Silver Spires
Princess at Silver Spires
Secrets at Silver Spires
Star of Silver Spires

...all featuring the Amethyst dorm girls

Want to know more about **School Friends**?
Check out
www.silverspiresschool.co.uk

Success
at
Silver
Spires

Ann Bryant

USBORNE

For Penny Senior with best wishes and grateful
thanks for all your invaluable help!

First published in the UK in 2010 by Usborne Publishing Ltd.,
Usborne House, 83-85 Saffron Hill, London EC1N 8RT, England.
www.usborne.com

Cover illustration by Rui Ricardo for folioart.co.uk

The name Usborne and the devices ♔ ☻ are Trade Marks of
Usborne Publishing Ltd.

This is a work of fiction. The characters, incidents, and dialogues are
products of the author's imagination and are not to be construed as real. Any
resemblance to actual events or persons, living or dead, is entirely coincidental.

A CIP catalogue record for this book is available from the British Library.

JFMAMJJASON /09 95199 ISBN 9780746098684
Printed in Reading, Berkshire, UK.

Chapter One

"**C**an you help with my stupid hair, Sasha?" said Emily, sighing dramatically.

I was the only one ready, so I jumped up from the bench in the changing rooms where we were sitting, and took the hairband she was holding out to me. It was going to be quite a challenge getting Emily's thick wavy hair squeezed into the small, thin band. No wonder she was having problems.

My best friend, Izzy, pulled a scrunchie out of her pocket. "Try this, Sash." And when I'd just about managed to make a fairly neat but rather stubby ponytail for Emily, Mrs. Truman, the PE teacher, clapped her hands, calling us all to attention.

It was the first PE lesson of the summer term and we knew things might be different from the last two terms. There's always so much going on at Silver Spires – it's just the best boarding school ever.

"Okay, girls, let's have a bit of hush and I'll tell you about the sport on offer in the summer."

Bryony and Emily, who are also in my close group of friends, gave each other quick, excited looks, as though they were dying to hear the news, and I thought how great it must be to be able to get excited about something like sport. I'm just not a sporty person, so whatever Mrs. Truman was about to say, it somehow didn't feel like it had anything to do with me.

"I think you're all going to find something to suit you this term," she began, as though she'd been reading my mind, "even those among you who think yourselves less sporty. The main two new activities that we're starting now are athletics and tennis…"

A bit of a cheer went up across the changing room, and I saw two girls clutching each other's hands as if they couldn't wait to get started. Bryony and Emily exchanged another bright-eyed look, so I took a quick glance at Izzy, but her expression didn't show any particular excitement.

She just seemed to be waiting for Mrs. Truman to carry on, like I was.

"Athletics includes anything that we do down on the athletics field, where we're going in a few minutes. There's high jump, long jump, triple jump and track events, such as short and long distance running, and, of course, hurdling."

Quite a few girls started whispering about what they liked best, and Mrs. Truman had to raise her voice a bit. "As I said, there is also an opportunity to play tennis this term, but there are other very different sports on offer too. So, listen carefully, and see if anything takes your fancy. Remember, though, if you decide to do one of the weekend courses, it's a proper commitment. You can't just start off and then quit part way through." Mrs. Truman looked stern for a moment, then carried on breezily. "Now, firstly, there's a sculling course, which is a kind of rowing, and that takes place on Saturday afternoons and Sunday mornings over three weekends before the half-term holiday, with a one-off mid-week session in the middle..."

"I'm definitely going to do that!" a girl called Holly said. Then she turned to her friend, Mikki, and I heard her say something about rowing with her brother at home.

"Or there's a sailing course," Mrs. Truman went on, "which is also over three weekends, but in the second half of term. And then there are two mountain-biking courses, one this half term, and one next. And lastly, for those of you who want a bit more adventure, there are a few additional one-day canoeing courses."

"Yea!" said a girl called Sophie from across the changing room. "Sounds great!" And quite a few other girls agreed.

Mrs. Truman smiled. "It's important to think carefully before signing up for anything. You girls lead very busy lives here at Silver Spires, with all your extra-curricular activities on top of your lessons, so don't overload yourselves." She smiled again. "On the other hand, there's a lot of enjoyment to be had out of sport, and you're amazingly lucky to have so much on offer..."

"Is the sculling a beginner's course?" asked Holly.

Mrs. Truman nodded. "Yes, it is." And I saw Holly's face drop.

I think Mrs. Truman must have noticed that too. "But there are seven sessions in all, so there's lots of chance to progress. The first one takes place here at the school swimming pool, then the others are at a lake not far away. Have you done sculling before, Holly?"

"I went out loads on the river with my brother over the Easter holidays. He's in a sculling eight but we went out together, just him and me, in a Virus double. It was great."

I looked round my group of friends to see if any of them seemed at all confused, but none of them did. So maybe I was the only one who didn't know the difference between sculling and rowing, and had no idea what a "Virus double" was, though it sounded like some kind of illness.

"He let me cox one time, too," Holly went on enthusiastically.

"What's that?" asked Bryony, and I felt relieved that at least one other person was in the dark. Bryony is Emily's best friend and she never wastes words.

"The cox—" Mrs. Truman started to answer, but Holly interrupted.

"It's the person who sits at the stern of the boat – that's the back – facing the way the boat's moving, so they can direct all the oarsmen to help them keep together and go as fast as possible."

"Well explained, Holly!" said Mrs. Truman. I agreed it was well explained but I still didn't understand what she'd said before about "viruses". I'm not like Bryony though. I'd never dare ask. Mrs. Truman was carrying on anyway, so I didn't have a chance to ask, even if I'd wanted to. "All the info about the various activities is on the sport noticeboard, so go along and sign up for whatever you want when you've had a good think about it.

"And one more important thing," she added. "General fitness. Up till now you've only used the main gym for PE lessons and dance, but if you want to use the equipment in the smaller gym to build up stamina – the treadmills, the bikes, the rowing machine, et cetera, that's fine. But you can *only* use that gym once you've had an induction, which is an introductory session to show you how to use the various pieces of equipment safely. Even then," she went on, "there has to be a member of staff with you at all times. And I'm afraid you're absolutely not allowed to use the weights, under any circumstances. But if it's raining outside, for example, and you want to work on your general fitness, that's where the gym comes in." Mrs. Truman smiled around at us, as if to see what we thought so far, but everyone was quiet and thoughtful. "The best time to use the gym is after school," she carried on, "though one or two older students sometimes try to squash in a session before breakfast, as long as it's after seven thirty. I'm afraid teachers get priority before that. But now –" she gave us another bright smile – "let's get down to the athletics field!"

Izzy and I found ourselves practically at the back as everyone else broke into excited chatter and plunged after Mrs. Truman. It's not that we don't like PE, just that it's not our favourite thing. Izzy's favourite thing is ballet, definitely. She's totally brilliant at it. And my favourite thing is...I don't know. I haven't got one. There's nothing I'm specially good at, really. I wish there was. It must be fantastic to be talented at something you also enjoy doing, like Izzy is.

I love the time of day when prep has finished and we're free for half an hour before we have to get ready for bed. Prep is like homework, except that we're not at home, of course, we're all in a big room and we have to work silently for about an hour. There's so much to get used to at a boarding school, but now that we Year Sevens have been here for two whole terms we feel completely settled.

As soon as prep was over that night, the six of us

went up to our dormitory, which is called Emerald. All the Year Seven dorms are named after precious stones, but we've got the best one. Actually, I think we've got the best boarding house too – Forest Ash. The boarding houses are named after trees, and Forest Ash sounds warm and friendly to me. Our housemistress is Mrs. Pridham. She's very gentle and kind, but can also be firm at times. And our matron is Miss Callow. She's really good fun. Then there's Miss Stevenson, the assistant housemistress, who is the youngest of the Forest Ash staff, and although she's the quietist and can be quite strict, everyone gets along well with her.

"I was a bit rubbish at that maths prep," said Emily with an over-the-top sigh, as she climbed the ladder to her cabin bed and lay down, hands behind her head. "I just don't get fractions." Then she turned onto her side and looked at Nicole, who is definitely the brainiest one of us all. "Tell me again, does the nominator go on the top in fractions, or is it the denumerator?"

Nicole laughed as she went up to sit with Antonia on her bed. "Oh, Ems, it's the *numerator* on the top, and *denominator* on the bottom!"

"Never mind maths," said Antonia, smiling round at us all. "What I want to know is which extra sports you have chosen. Nicole and I have signed in for tennis."

"Signed *up*," said Nicole straight away. Then she looked apologetic. "Sorry, Antonia! You must get sick of me correcting you all the time!"

Antonia shook her head. "I want to be just as good as all of you at English, so keep correcting me till I am!"

"You *are* as good as us!" I told Antonia, because I think it's brilliant the way she's learned English in only two terms. Last September, when we joined Silver Spires, she couldn't really speak it at all and had a strong Italian accent, but now she's great at it, and has practically lost her accent too.

"Well, anyway, Nicole and I are going to do extra tennis!" she told us happily.

"I don't think we'll exactly make Wimbledon, this year," said Nicole. "But we're really looking forward to it all the same!" Then she turned to Bryony. "What are you going to do, Bry?"

"She's coming riding with me," Emily answered. "Which is totally brave of her because..." Emily stopped suddenly and clapped her hand over her mouth. "Sorry, Bry, is it a secret?"

Bryony shrugged. "Because I'm scared of horses," she said in a matter-of-fact voice.

Izzy gasped. "I didn't think you were scared of *anything*, Bry!"

And I didn't either because Bryony has been on all sorts of outward-bound trips over the year, like abseiling and rock climbing, and you need tons of courage for those.

"I fell off a horse when I was little," she told us quietly. "And I've never got back on one since, but now I'm going to give it a go."

"We won't have time for anything else though, with gardening club and everything," finished off Emily simply. Then she turned to me and Izzy. "What about you two?"

I suddenly felt a bit pathetic for having no idea. "I don't know. There are so many things…" I was trying to make it sound as though I was interested in everything and just couldn't choose, but the truth was I didn't think I'd be that good at any of the things on offer.

"We can't decide, can we, Sash?" Izzy added, pulling her hair out of its band and starting to brush it.

I was glad at that moment not to be the only one who wasn't really sporty. But immediately afterwards I felt miserable, because of course even though Izzy isn't sporty, she's always got ballet as her special thing in life, and I really admire her dedication to it. And all the others have something that's important to them too. Emily's big passion is the environment. Bryony is the adventurous one, Nicole got a scholarship to Silver Spires because she's so clever, and Antonia is a brilliant linguist and knows more about the world than any of us because she's travelled such a lot. Then there's me. I really feel like a nobody.

When my parents told me last summer that I was definitely coming to Silver Spires, the very first thing I thought was that I might find something here that I could shine at, or at least something I'd really enjoy. But that just hasn't happened.

It's not that I'm unhappy. I'm completely happy, because this is the best boarding school in the world, and I've got my five close friends, including my very best friend, and I'm quite good at all the different lessons, and quite good at everything in fact. It's just that I'm a *quite good* sort of person, who'd love to be a *very good* sort of person at *something*.

I sighed inside and tried to get back to thinking about extra sports, and there suddenly flashed through my mind the memory of that girl, Holly, talking about sculling with her brother. She sounded like she'd really had fun with him. I wished I had a big brother instead of baby twin brothers – someone who might teach me to be a *very* sort of person instead of a *quite* one.

"We could always try sculling," I found myself saying to Izzy before I'd really thought it through.

"Y-yes..." said Izzy, looking doubtful. "Do you think it's hard?"

"Have you ever done sculling, Bry?" I asked her. "What's the difference between sculling and rowing?"

"Each person on a rowing team uses just one oar, but in sculling they use two," said Bryony. "I only know that from watching the Olympic Games, by the way."

"You ought to give it a go, Sash!" said Emily.

I turned to Izzy. "*Shall* we?" I asked, a bit nervously.

She hunched her shoulders up and pulled a face. "I'm not sure. I keep remembering what Mrs. Truman said about it being a commitment. I mean, what if we don't like it?"

"Or what if we're no good at it?" I added quietly, because that was what was worrying me.

"Stop worrying, Sasha, and go for it! You might turn out to be *fantastico*!" laughed Nicole, using one of the Italian words she'd learned from Antonia.

"*Shall* we?" This time it was Izzy asking me.

I suddenly pictured myself phoning home to tell Mum and Dad what brilliant fun sculling was, and Dad wanting to know every detail about it, then Mum trying to get the phone off him so she could hear too. In my heart I knew that wouldn't happen because Dad's always working and Mum's attention is totally taken up by the twins. Maybe if I tried out something new, though, she'd be really curious and ask me lots of questions about it. I liked that thought.

Izzy was looking at me, her head on one side, waiting for my answer. I made the decision in a flash.

"Yes, let's!" I said a bit breathlessly.

The very next day Izzy and I signed up for sculling, then, as Saturday drew nearer, I found myself getting more and more tense, because there was no going back. A very small part of me was excited, but most of me was nervous and anxious. Why was *I*, of all people, about to take up sculling, when I'd no real idea what it actually was? Izzy felt the same, thank goodness, and we would keep turning to each other during the school day – like in the dinner queue, in the middle of a lesson, walking out of assembly, or while we were cleaning our teeth – and saying, "What if we're useless at it?" and "What if we hate it?"

But then we always finished up reminding ourselves that Holly had talked about scull doubles, and that as long as we were together in a boat for two people, surely it would be good fun.

Then Saturday afternoon finally arrived, and I was more nervous than ever in the swimming pool changing room, with Izzy and the rest of the fifteen Year Sevens and Eights who'd signed up for sculling. Mrs. Truman had told us to put our costumes on underneath cycling shorts and a T-shirt. Someone had already asked her why we had to wear cycling shorts rather than any old shorts, and she'd said it was so they wouldn't get caught on any parts of the boat. That was the moment when it had all started to sound very real to me.

"You're going to get a bit of a shock when you see what's in the pool," she said, wearing a kind of secretive smile. "Come on, girls, quick as you can."

We knew there would be some kind of a boat in the pool because Mrs. Truman had already mentioned that, but when we walked through from the changing room, every single one of us gasped.

There, floating in the middle of the pool, was a long, very, very slim, gleaming white boat. It looked as though the slightest breath of wind would tip it over.

Instantly I knew there was no way I was ever going to be able to manage this sport. I must have been mad even to consider it.

Chapter Two

"**D**on't look so terrified!" came a man's voice. "Gather round, girls!"

It was hard dragging my eyes from the beautiful but scary-looking boat to the man who seemed to be in charge. He was wearing a dark blue polo shirt and a pair of combats that went down to just below the knee and his feet were bare. He seemed very young to be a teacher but I'm not very good at ages. Straight away he told us that his name was Ryan. That's all he told us, though, before he suddenly fell into the pool.

Another huge gasp filled the pool area and I

snatched a glance at Mrs. Truman and the other two ladies who I noticed were also standing on the side. Not one of them moved at all – not even a twitch – which made me think that Ryan must have fallen in on purpose. But I could see quite a few girls who were still looking shocked and others who were laughing.

A moment later he heaved himself out of the pool, dripping wet but smiling all over his face. "There you are, girls. Falling in is nothing to worry about. That's the first lesson. So *what* if you've got all your clothes on? Yes, it might be a bit cold, but there's no need to dwell on that – you just need to think *safety*. So, let's get started. My name's Ryan, as I said, and I'm from the Pollington Water Sports Club. Here's our logo!" He tapped the red and pale blue picture on his shirt. It seemed to be of two trees growing towards each other on an island in the middle of a lake. But when I looked closely I saw that the trees were actually a pair of oars with a sail in the middle. "This is Celia, and this is Penny," he went on, introducing the two ladies, who were also wearing dark blue polo shirts with the same logo, only they had shorts on rather than combats.

"Hi!" they said, giving us a little wave.

I thought they looked really nice and friendly, and a little of my nervousness dissolved – but only a little. We'd not started the session yet and I had no idea how on earth anyone was expected to balance in such a narrow boat that didn't even have a flat bottom. And worse, it looked like you had to sit *on* it, not *in* it.

"Right we're here today to learn what to do if ever you should happen to…fall in." He gave a little chuckle. "Which is most unlikely, because the boats you learn in are sturdier than this. We call this the capsize drill. It's something we have to practise before we set out on the lake and start sculling properly. I'm going to choose five people to stay here and work with me and Celia on that, while the rest of you go off to the shallow end with Penny. Then we'll swap to another five and so on. Now, I've already checked with Mrs. Truman and I know you're all good, confident swimmers so it doesn't matter who I choose. Right…" He was looking over the heads of the people at the front to the ones at the back, like me and Izzy. I tried to shrink away from his gaze so he wouldn't pick me, but it didn't work. I was the first one he pointed to, and Izzy was the second. Then there were three Year Eights – Kerry, Rhianna and Poppy.

Penny gathered everyone else around her and they went off to the shallow end. Izzy and I exchanged scared looks and I think Ryan must have noticed, because he quickly told us there was nothing to worry about, and that the boats we were going to use at Pollington Water were called stable sculls. "That means it's pretty much impossible to fall in," he grinned, "as they've got flat bottoms! We're only practising in this racing scull because it's so much easier to turn over."

"So will we be in stable boats for the whole course?" asked Poppy.

"Probably, yes, because it's most unusual to progress to a racing boat in the short amount of training that you'll be having. Although some of you might move on from Virus singles to a double for two people, or quad scull for four. And in case you're wondering, 'Virus' is just the make of the boat."

Izzy and I exchanged an anxious look. We'd been so sure we'd be sculling together in a double boat. But we had to quickly put that thought out of our minds and concentrate on what Ryan was doing. He was back in the water, and a moment later, with what seemed like no effort at all, he'd got himself into the boat. At exactly the same time there came a loud splash, followed by a lot of laughter from the shallow end, and I was aware of everyone around me looking over to see what was happening. But I wasn't interested. I couldn't take my eyes off the oars that rested gently on the water at either side of the beautiful racing scull, like they were part of it.

"Right," began Ryan, "I've got my feet in the special shoes which are attached to the boat, and I'm just going to throw away the blades – or oars, if that's what you prefer to call them – then immediately hold on tight to the riggers, which are the metal bits on the side of the boat. And once the boat has rolled over, I'll slip my feet out of the shoes. Here we go!" He did exactly as he'd said and we watched him go right under for just a couple of seconds, then quickly come up and loop his arm over the upturned boat.

My heart was beating faster as I tried to understand the feeling that was coming over me. I couldn't work out if I was really scared or really excited, but I thought it might be a mixture of both.

"Have we all got to do *that*?" asked Kerry, which made one or two people laugh.

"Yes!" said Ryan plainly. "But just for now we are going to work with this upturned boat, okay?" His expression became much more serious as he continued. "Now, if you're near the side of the lake when you fall in, the obvious thing to do would be simply to tow the boat in, and it's much easier if it's the right way up. But imagine you're far away from the side. One option would be to right the boat, get back in and row back. Can anyone think of a reason why you might *not* right the boat, though?"

Ryan was looking around at us waiting to see if anyone knew the answer, when the shape of the upturned boat that was right before my eyes in the middle of our pool gave me an idea. But I didn't think I dared to speak in case it was stupid. If only I could whisper it to Izzy first to see what she thought... So I leaned towards her – and Ryan spotted me straight away.

"Girl with the blue eyes...what do you think?" He was smiling at me in a kind way, so I plucked up all my courage and decided to risk it.

"Er...is it easier to cling to the boat when it's upside down?"

"Absolutely! Well done...er?"

He was waiting for me to say my name. "Sasha."

"Good answer, Sasha. And why might you cling to the boat rather than getting back in?"

"Because you might be too scared or hurt or something," answered Kerry.

"That's right," said Ryan.

"And if anyone was watching, they'd realize you were in trouble when they saw the upside-down boat," added Rhianna.

As Rhianna had been talking I was imagining how freezing cold and frightening it would be to be stuck clinging to your upturned boat far from the side of a lake, and I did a little shiver just at the thought of it.

"Good!" said Ryan to Rhianna. "And if possible you should try to get out of the water and on top of the upturned boat. Why is that?" His eyes swept over us again, and I quickly answered before I had time to worry that I might not be right.

"Because the water would be so cold...I mean colder than the air."

"Yes, absolutely. And it's important to keep your body temperature up. Well done! Actually you can do a kind of surf paddle with your hands while you're lying on top of the boat, but for now let's just get you used to climbing onto it. Only before *that*, we need you all in the water." He rubbed his hands. "You can jump in, if you're feeling confident, or slither in, if you want the torture method!"

We looked at each other and shivered, then every single one of us sat down on the side ready to slide ourselves in.

"Come on, girls! Be brave!" said Celia, jumping in with a big splash to set a good example.

No one took up her challenge, though, and I wondered whether Ryan and Celia thought we were a bit of a pathetic lot. They'd probably done this drill at loads of schools, and I didn't want them going away thinking that Silver Spires was for wimps. If only Bryony had been with us, she would have jumped in and not even thought about it.

The water seemed cold at first and it felt funny wearing clothes in the pool, so we all started treading water frantically, while we watched Celia demonstrating how to climb onto the upturned boat.

"Okay, Sasha, you go first!" she said as she slithered off. "Don't worry, Ryan will keep the boat steady if you need him, and I'm here to help too."

I felt quite nervous to start with, because I was certain I was going to wobble around or fall in, but surprisingly I managed to scramble on straight away without Ryan or Celia helping me, and the moment I was lying on my tummy on top of that boat, I felt a lovely thrill, as though something had clicked in place inside me.

"Fantastic!" said Ryan, giving me a friendly grin. "Who's next?"

So one at a time the other four did exactly what I'd just done, but I felt so proud because no one seemed to manage it quite so easily as I had.

"You were great," said Izzy when she'd had her turn. "It took me loads longer than you!"

"Okay, now I'm going to turn the boat the right way up and you can take turns towing it to the side," said Ryan. "Listen to Celia."

"The front of the scull is called the bow," she said, pronouncing "bow" to rhyme with "cow". "And this is the end you should hold firmly, like this, with two hands." She was lying on her back. "Now watch how I use a kind of kicking action, a bit like treading water... See how my head stays clear of the water so I can keep a look out." She stayed in that position as she towed the boat to the side. Then she guided it gently back to the middle, and asked me to be the first to have a go again.

I swam up to the boat, then suddenly started worrying. Desperate to get my turn over with, I quickly grabbed the front – I mean the bow – trying to imitate Celia's demonstration. I heaved myself up with a big kick, so my head was well out of the water and I could see over the boat. And, finally, I kicked my legs and started moving back towards the side of the pool, clinging on hard to the boat with my hands.

"Well, that was absolutely brilliant!" said Celia. "You seem like a complete natural, Sasha. You didn't need me at all! Well done!"

I'd been feeling cold, but Celia's words warmed me up more than the hottest sun could have done. I was so relieved and happy that I'd managed to do the first two exercises right, *and* Celia thought I was a natural. I couldn't wait to tell Mum and Dad! But a moment later I felt guilty for only thinking about my own success, because it was Izzy's turn now and she was really struggling to get the boat moving the right way.

"I was hopeless," she said through her shivers, as she swam over and clung to the side with me. I put my arm round her and told her she was fine.

"Well done, all of you!" said Ryan after the three Year Eights had had their turns. "Off you go to the shallow end, and then, when the other two groups have had a go, we'll bring you lot back for the full capsize."

Holly was one of the group that had their turn after us, and, while we were having fun with Penny at the shallow end, I couldn't help noticing how Holly was getting on with the same moves that we'd just done. As I expected, she managed everything really easily and got lots of praise from Celia and

Ryan. But then, when everyone from her group had had a turn and they were about to swap to the last group of girls, Holly asked when they were actually going to practise capsizing.

"All in good time," said Ryan.

Holly nodded but she looked a bit sulky as her group swapped places and came to join the rest of us. We were diving for coins at the bottom of the pool. Penny had thrown them in because she wanted to see how well we could hold our breath underwater.

When Ryan finally announced that the moment we'd all been waiting for had arrived, I felt my old nervousness creeping back.

"First group back here please for the capsizing of the boat!" he called and we swam towards the deep end, where we clung anxiously to the side, muttering about how scared we were. But Ryan cut through all our nervous chatter. "Okay, watch carefully while I do another quick demo."

I noticed again how smoothly he got himself into the scull without Celia steadying it for him, and held onto the oars – I mean, blades – so easily. Then he kept his balance as he explained to us that he was going to pretend to lose control.

"Remember that the first thing is to release the

blades, and then hold on tight to the riggers. Then you'll roll into the water and go under and you can slide your feet out of the shoes and pop back up again. Now this time I want you to imagine you're in rough water, so you'll need to cling to the boat before it gets swept away. Notice how, once I've gone under and come up again, I grab onto the boat as soon as I can. Okay, here we go!"

Ryan threw away the blades just like the last time, rolled the scull over and, in what seemed like no time at all, he'd popped back up to the surface and looped his arm over the upturned boat. "Right, let's start with Sasha again. Celia will help you to get in, Sasha, and I'll be steadying the scull."

Celia smiled and held out her hand to me, then she showed me exactly where to place both my hands and how to push down against the top of the boat to lift myself out of the water. After that, I knew I had to swing my feet in and kind of lift myself as best I could onto the seat. I was very tense and felt as though I was using all my strength, but, incredibly, I managed it first go. Celia said I did it amazingly well, which sent another little surge of pride whizzing through me.

"That's it, now get hold of the blades," she said.

"And in a moment I'm going to let go of the

boat," Ryan called to me. "Stay calm, just let go of the blades and hold on, then get your feet out of the shoes once you've rolled over and fallen in. Celia will be there if you need her. Here we go then!"

I was bracing myself, all ready to roll into the water the second Ryan let go – and then he *had*, and yet I wasn't rolling. The boat seemed to be staying upright. I felt absolutely brilliant.

"Nice one!" called Ryan.

But from the other end of the pool came Holly's loud voice. "It's not that hard to balance when the blades are resting on the water." And it was as though her words had broken a spell, because I suddenly felt as though I was losing my balance and a second later I found myself in the water. I'd let go of the blades and released my feet from the shoes without even realizing, and I was coming up to the surface. Gasping for breath, straight away I grabbed the boat, and that's when I heard clapping.

"Well done, Sasha!" called Izzy from the side.

Ryan did a big whoop. "Excellent stuff, Sasha. Good work!"

I had never blushed so deeply. It felt fantastic.

* * *

In our dorm that night we all lay in bed and talked for ages after we'd turned our lights out. We often whisper in the dark, once the person on duty has popped her head round the door to tell us it's time for lights out, and then been round a few minutes later to check we've done it. Tonight we were trying to cheer Izzy up, because she hadn't really enjoyed anything during the session in the pool, and I felt really sorry for her.

"You were so good and I was so rubbish," she wailed.

"No you weren't!" I kept telling her. "Anyway, remember, Ryan said that there's no way we can fall out of the flat-bottomed stable sculls, so you won't have to worry about that tomorrow."

Izzy seemed to cheer up after that, and we were all quiet for a while. Personally, I was thinking about the phone call I'd had with Dad before we'd had to hand our mobiles in to Matron. Mum had been putting the twins to bed, so I'd spoken to Dad for ages, telling him all about the capsize drill and how well I'd done. I was dying to tell Mum too, but she was so long with the twins that in the end Dad promised she'd phone me back the next day.

"Shall I tell her what you've told me, or would you rather tell her yourself tomorrow, Sash?"

"It's okay, you can tell her, Dad."

"Well, she'll be really pleased, I'm sure."

I did want her to be pleased, of course, but more than that I wanted her to be really interested and maybe a bit proud of me. But then, when I came to think about it, there was nothing for her to feel proud about really. All I'd done was to survive the first session of the course and not let myself down too badly. It was nothing great, it just felt great to me, because I'd been so worried about it.

"Holly was good, wasn't she?" came Izzy's sleepy voice from the semi darkness.

I thought back to the way Holly had rolled the scull so easily when her group had finally had a go at capsizing, just as though she was playing with a toy.

"Yes, she was great."

And then I imagined us all out on Pollington Water in our stable sculls the next day, and a part of me couldn't help feeling a bit sad that I wouldn't be in one of those beautiful racing sculls. That thought made me smile. Something had changed inside me. The racing scull didn't fill me with fear any more. It filled me with...excitement. And ambition.

Chapter Three

I woke up really early on Sunday. It was as though my mind was prodding me out of my sleep, saying, *Remember, this is the day when you're going to get your first proper taste of sculling!*

Emily, as usual, was already up. On Sundays we always have a lie-in because it's the one day of the week when there aren't any lessons. But, even on Sundays, Emily seems to wake up early. She says it's because she's lived on a farm all her life and can't break the habit of getting up to help with the milking.

"I'm going to the garden," she said, rushing off.

"See you at breakfast, Sash."

Emily is never still for a moment. She hates flopping about and chilling more than anyone I know. When she's got any free time, she's always outside gardening or just breathing in the fresh air, because she's so used to the big open spaces in Ireland where she comes from.

Last night Bryony, Nicole and Antonia told me they planned to have a lovely lie-in this morning, then after breakfast they were going to take Mrs. Pridham's advice. "Silver Spires is so beautiful in the summer term," she'd said, "go and have a wander round Pets' Place and down to the athletics field. Explore the back of the boarding houses or sit on the grassy slope behind the main building. There's a wonderful view across the countryside from there."

But now it was only seven o'clock in the morning and I had to wait till nine o'clock before we'd be setting off to Pollington Water. I wished I hadn't woken up so early. There was nothing to do except feel nervous while I was waiting.

"What time is it?" Izzy was sitting bolt upright, looking really anxious.

"It's okay, Iz, I just happened to wake up early. Go back to sleep."

"I don't think I'll be able to sleep now. I'm too nervous. Let's get up and go to breakfast, shall we?"

"Pollington Water, here we come!" said Mrs. Ansell, the housemistress of Willowhaven, turning on the minibus ignition.

We students were all chatting and laughing and being what Mrs. Ansell called "Far too high for your own good!"

"We're just excited!" one of the Year Eights pointed out.

"Yes, well save it for when you get there!" was Mrs. Ansell's dry reply. "Final check – has everyone got spare clothing?"

We all called out, "Yes, Mrs. Ansell!"

Then off we went. The journey went quite quickly as we all chatted away noisily, but when we got our first view of Pollington Water, the noise suddenly stopped for a few seconds, then turned into gasps and oohs and aahs, because Pollington Water was so beautiful. For a start the lake was absolutely massive, with an island in the middle. In the distance we could see sailing boats, like tiny white flags dancing in the wind, and balls of different colours, which must have been buoys, bobbing over the surface.

It was a lovely day, with blue sky and bright sun making the water look like rippled blue-grey velvet. And all around the lake were big stretches of green grass and trees and shrubs with a few people walking their dogs or just strolling with their families.

"I wish I'd brought my camera," breathed Izzy.

I really loved the atmosphere and was surprised to find myself itching to get out onto the water. But the feeling didn't last long. As we pulled into the car park, and drew closer to the water, my old nervousness started pouring back, clogging up my whole body. Izzy and I were the only quiet ones. Everyone else was jumping up and down with excitement as they got off the minibus, talking loudly about how cool it was going to be. And Holly even rushed to the nearest stretch of grass and did a cartwheel. "I love it here!" she said. "I feel as though it's where I belong!"

Her friend, Mikki, laughed happily. "You're mad, Holly!"

But I thought it was brilliant that she felt so enthusiastic. I wished I could be like her. Why did I always have to worry and feel so nervous every time I came across anything new in my life?

Ryan, Celia and Penny met us at the boathouse

and introduced us to two other coaches, George and Ben.

"You'll be working in groups of three and each group will have one of us coaches," said Ryan. Then he told us to have a wander round the boathouse and look at the Virus singles, doubles and quads. "I think you're going to be surprised, girls, when you see how robust the boats are. We might use the doubles or quads later in the course, but you all need to get used to the singles first. They're much easier, because you don't have to worry about keeping your strokes in time with anyone else when you're sculling."

My heart sank and I glanced across at Izzy. She looked as disappointed as I felt. We'd both still been hoping we could scull together, but we'd just have to wait for that chance.

Holly scarcely glanced inside the door. "I've been in the boathouse at my brother's rowing club loads of times," she said.

Everyone else took their cue from Holly, appearing totally confident and excited and just having a quick look, apart from a group of Year Eights who seemed as anxious as me and Izzy. The three of them went right inside the boathouse, looking at the single sculls and whispering to each other about how they thought they'd probably be all right, as the bottoms of the boats were definitely nice and flat. I heard one of them say very quietly, "Don't worry, Beth, there's no way you're going to fall in."

"Look, Sasha, they've all got names," said Izzy.

I'd noticed that too, and was wondering who all those names belonged to and whether they were even real people. "*Sandy Phillipson*," I read out loud. "*Carla Conrad*."

Eventually Izzy and I realized we were the only two people left in the boathouse, still looking at all the names of the boats. "*Gary Ferris*, and this one's just got one name," said Izzy. "Look. *Annalisa*."

"Okay, let's get to work!"

We turned to see Ryan and Ben getting hold of one of the Virus singles. "Let's get some of these down to the water, shall we?" They carried the boat on its side out of the boathouse and we followed them and joined the others.

"You see how we're carrying the boats?" said Ryan. He and Ben took a few more steps while we all watched silently, then Ben put his end down and went back into the boathouse, calling to Holly to come and help him with the next boat.

Ryan pointed to Kerry. "Can you come and take Ben's place please?" he said.

Then the other three coaches each chose a girl to help them, and told the rest of us to collect the buoyancy aids. Celia explained that the buoyancy aids are like life jackets but they're inflated all the time so you don't have to do anything to them once you're in the water. They looked to me as though they'd cover you up more than a life jacket would too, and Celia said it was true that in the cold or the rain, they keep you warmer and drier. Izzy and I each carried an extra one for two of the girls carrying sculls.

"I'm scared," said Izzy suddenly.

"Me too," I whispered back. "Everyone else seems so excited though, don't they?"

The coaches got the five boats into the water, then divided us into groups of three. I was with Izzy and a girl called Chloe, and Celia was our coach.

First we had to learn about locking the blades in place by fastening up metal pieces called gates on either side of the boat. Celia demonstrated the gate on the landing-stage side first, then she got in the boat and did up the gate on the water side. She asked us each to have a go. Izzy was a bit scared about leaning over the water but everyone managed all right in the end.

Next Celia got in the boat again and showed us how to adjust the foot stretcher where we had to rest our feet. "See how you can move it forwards if you're a taller person or backwards if you're smaller? That's so you can get it into the comfiest position for your height, then stick the Velcro straps down. You'll know you're in the correct position when you sit with your legs straight and the two oar handles against your stomach are about a fist width apart, see?"

Again, we watched carefully and then all had a turn. Surprisingly, I was chosen to go first again, and Celia praised me for getting it right straight away. I was expecting to feel wobbly in the boat, especially when Celia let go, but I surprised myself by feeling fine. "Hold the handles of the oars with your thumbs on the ends...that's right, Sasha. Good!"

Once we were used to getting in and out of the boat, Celia said she wanted us to feel how the boat rocked, and the others seemed happy for me to go first yet again, after Celia's demonstration. I had to push the oar handles down onto what Celia called their "legs", and hold them there, then I had to use my body to rock the boat from side to side so that the oars splashed the water. With the Velcro straps holding my trainers in position, it wasn't as hard as I'd expected. I really enjoyed that bit, and I think the other groups were enjoying it too, because I could hear lots of laughter all around me.

After Izzy and Chloe had had their turns, Celia said it was time to take a stroke. She tied one end of a rope to the back of my boat – whoops, I should be calling it the stern, not the back – and held on to the other end. "Now you might feel a bit like a dog on a lead," she said, smiling at me, "but this means that I can help pull you out of the way of other boats to avoid too many crashes!" And just as she said the word "crashes" we heard a shriek from someone in Ben's group who'd crashed into another boat. "See what I mean!" laughed Celia.

It was good to know that she was guiding me and calling out instructions from the side, because I still felt nervous while I was learning how to sit and exactly how to position the oars.

"That's right," said Celia, encouraging me, "now push your hands down so the oars are out of the water, straighten your arms keeping the oars out…" There was so much to remember but once I'd done six or seven strokes I really felt as though I'd got it. The only odd thing is that it feels like you're going backwards as you're sculling along, because the front, or bow of the boat, is behind you leading the way, while *you* are actually facing the back, or stern of the boat.

"Yes, that's great!" said Celia, watching me. "I'm going to take the rope off and let you paddle on alone, Sasha. By the way, I'll always talk about *paddling on* when I want you to go forwards as you are now. And then we'll learn how to *back it down*, which is when the scull is going backwards."

When Celia untied the rope from my boat it felt absolutely brilliant to be sculling on my own, and I realized, with a lovely lurch of happiness, that for once I wasn't even nervous.

"Just turn your head occasionally to check your direction," called Celia. "Try to keep... Oh! Well done, Sasha! I was going to say try to keep in a straight line, but you're doing it automatically!"

And I was. It just felt so natural and brilliant, with the wind in my face and my arms guiding the blades to make them slice smoothly through the water. Only one other boat had come as far away from the land as mine, and with a quick sideways glance I saw that it was Holly, and wondered if she felt the same as I did as she sculled along, all strong and free.

"Nice work, Holly!" called Ryan.

Then Celia gave me instructions for turning the

scull round. "First check it's safe to turn... Okay, now I'd like you to take strokes with your left hand, so organize the right hand first. Put the blade flat on the water and hold it into your turning so it's out of the way... That's right...and lean slightly into it. Now get ready to paddle with your left hand. Make sure it's square...." It all felt so natural. "Good, those are nice long strokes, that's why you're turning quickly." And when I realized I'd done it, my heart sang.

After me, Izzy had her turn. Watching from the side I could see that lots of people were having problems with their stroke action and couldn't really get going, but everyone was clearly enjoying themselves, all the same. Mrs. Ansell had been for a walk round the lake, but she'd come back and was watching us now. "Smile, Izzy. Let's have a photo for the website!"

"No, don't take a photo of me!" Izzy called. "I'm hopeless. Do Sasha!"

Holly was just getting out of her boat at that moment but she called out to Ryan, "Shall I quickly row out again so Mrs. Ansell can get an action shot, Ryan?"

"No, no, no. Don't worry about me!" laughed Mrs. Ansell. "I'm quite happy snapping away. There's plenty of time."

Holly looked really cross, and it didn't help that Izzy, who had been watching the conversation, suddenly lost her concentration and even though she was still on a rope her scull strayed just far enough to crash into Holly's by mistake. Then all Holly's anger was aimed at poor Izzy in the nastiest glare I've ever seen.

As soon as Izzy got out of the boat a few minutes later, I told her to ignore Holly.

"She's really good at it, though, isn't she?" said Izzy, sounding rather shaken. Then her voice dropped to a whisper. "But not as good as you, Sash. You're the best!"

I looked round to see why Izzy was whispering and realized that Holly was close by, leaning against a tree, looking bored. "There ought to be more boats out," she was saying in a hiss to Mikki. "It's boring watching other people learn."

I'm sure it was just a coincidence but, straight after she'd said that, Ryan suddenly shouted, "Right, George, let's get more boats out. There are quite a few girls who can manage on their own now."

"*I'm* not going on my own," Izzy said quietly to me. "I want to stay with Celia on the end of a rope. I feel safe like that."

* * *

46

Ten minutes later I was humming to myself as I started to scull towards the little island in the lake. I was leaving the laughter and chatter and splashes and crashes of the people near the side, and pulling out on my own, enjoying every stroke.

"That's great, Sasha!" called Celia, giving me a thumbs up. "You're keeping a nice straight line. I'll be along to join you in a second." She was climbing into a little inflatable dinghy.

I gave her a contented grin, but I wasn't sure she'd be able to see it. I was getting further and further away from land.

Celia rowed effortlessly towards me. At least it looked effortless. "You've got a great stroke action, Sasha," she said, as she pulled alongside me. "Now, see those buoys over there?" I turned to look at the orange floating balls. "Remember, they mark your limit, so you'll need to turn round when you get to them, just like you practised, then you can scull back. But if you feel like coming back at any time before that, that's fine. It's tiring work, when you first learn to scull!" She gave me a big smile. "I'll be keeping you in my sights, don't worry. Okay, off you go!"

So then I was on my own again. And it actually felt easy. It was amazing because I was the only one who'd sculled this far, although there was another scull approaching rapidly. And as it came nearer, I saw it was Holly. She whipped her head round, noticed me, then turned back again immediately, and I don't know if I imagined it, but she seemed to be rowing even more quickly after that, which made me think she was trying to catch me up.

The gap between us was definitely narrowing, but I surprised myself by feeling suddenly competitive and sculling harder, determined to keep ahead of Holly, and wishing my arms were more powerful, so I could really whizz across the water. I put more energy into the action then, finding exactly the right angle and depth for my blades to push against the water and pull me along with a whoosh.

Holly wasn't gaining on me any more now, and I turned quickly to see how much further I had to go before I reached the buoys. Now they were nearer I could see that they weren't actually shaped at all like balls. I suddenly wished I could go on and on, further and further, I was loving it so much. Every sound seemed just right to me at that moment – the bubbles rippling along the sides of the boat, birds singing somewhere high above me, and, best of all, the soft slap of the blades as they swished through the water. The island was only about fifty metres away, and each time I turned quickly to check I was going in the right direction, I glimpsed the green and brown of the trees and specks of white between them, which must have been the sailing boats we'd seen earlier on the other side of the island.

Suddenly Celia seemed to be spurting along towards me and I realized she'd got a little motor in her boat. "Well done!" she called out to Holly as she passed her. "That's a good confident stroke you've got there!"

"I've done it before, that's why," said Holly.

"Excellent." Celia watched her for a few more seconds. "Right, I want you and Sasha to turn round in a minute."

I slowed down then, and Holly caught up, so the three of us were all in a line, side by side, and it seemed suddenly very quiet because Celia had switched off her motor.

"I don't usually have to come out so far to get people to turn back on their first session! It's good to see such enthusiasm and natural ability from you two!"

Holly didn't say anything, she just turned neatly round. I wasn't quite so quick, because I went the wrong way at first. The boats turn so easily that you have to be careful not to overdo it. But Celia seemed happy with me.

"Nice work. Now if you two need me I'll be helping Izzy and Chloe, but if you're okay just to keep practising going backwards and forwards, that's great."

I couldn't have begun to tell her how okay I was, so I just nodded hard and smiled like mad as she switched her motor back on and went zooming over to the others, leaving Holly and me alone – two silent scullers in a big stretch of rippling blue-grey water.

Holly didn't look at me at first, but then just for the tiniest moment she glanced across. When our eyes met I gave her a smile, but she lowered her gaze immediately. My perfectly happy time felt somehow a bit less perfect because of that, though I tried not to let it bother me and just kept sculling away, stroke after stroke, concentrating on getting the best possible action. Our silence felt too uncomfortable, though, when we were alone together so far away from the others. I was just wishing I could think of something to say when the perfect thing popped into my head. "Have you noticed we're keeping exactly in time with each other, Holly?"

She didn't reply and neither did she smile, but a moment later I realized our strokes weren't in sync any more and Holly was pulling ahead. Why had she changed her rhythm as soon as I'd mentioned it? It might have been a coincidence. But something told me she'd done it on purpose, and it felt like Holly was the one thing spoiling this lovely day.

"Oh Holly, you're such a brilliant sculler!" It was Mikki's voice, and it made me realize how close we were to land. Most of the girls' sculls were still on ropes but a few others were on their own now. I caught sight of Izzy's tense pale face, but then a moment later she relaxed into a laugh when a Year Eight, called Georgie, crashed into her.

"Whoops! Sorry, Izzy! Haven't quite got the hang of it yet!"

I was glad that Izzy was managing to enjoy herself, even if sculling wasn't turning out to be her thing. Then I turned round at exactly the same time as Holly and we set off back towards the island. I didn't want to be near her now, though. It was too much of a strain. So I just sculled gently until she was well ahead.

"Whoa! I've got it, Ben! Look!" I heard another Year Eight call. I think her name was Charlotte. It was true, she was sculling really smoothly out towards me. She flicked her head round and broke into a grin when she saw me. "It's such good fun, isn't it!"

So then I slowed down even more and she came alongside me. For a while our strokes were exactly matching, and for some reason it seemed to make it easier to scull.

"Have you noticed," said Charlotte, as though she was reading my mind, "that when you're in time with another boat, it actually seems to help?"

"Yes, you're right," I replied, smiling to myself.

It was strange, but being in time with Charlotte felt so different from being in time with Holly. In one way I preferred it with Holly, because I moved faster and worked harder, which was an amazing feeling. But, on the other hand, it was an easy, friendly silence with Charlotte, and I could just tell she was enjoying herself.

"It's nice when you find you're good at something that you weren't expecting to be good at, isn't it?" she suddenly said.

I grinned and nodded, knowing exactly what she meant. And that was when I looked up and realized that Mrs. Ansell had taken a photo of us.

Chapter Four

On the way back to school in the minibus, my emotions got all mixed up. Most of me was feeling really happy that I'd enjoyed the morning so much. Charlotte's words were still buzzing away in my mind – *It's nice when you find you're good at something that you weren't expecting to be good at.* On the other hand, I could already feel my happiness seeping away, because I didn't think I could bear to wait for the next sculling session. At least it was only three days away, as there was a mid-week session on Wednesday.

But something else was tugging at my happiness. In a word, Holly.

"I don't think she likes me," I said to Izzy in a whisper.

"That's because she thought she was going to be the best sculler and get all the attention, and you've come along and spoiled everything!" Izzy replied. "I'm quite glad actually. She shouldn't be such a show-off!"

The main thing that was worrying me was that at the end of the session I'd heard Holly asking Ryan when she could go in a quad scull as she'd sculled before and didn't want to get bored. And she also asked if she could choose which people could go with her. She'd quickly added that she thought it should be Mikki, Charlotte, Tilly and Caitlin. I was a bit confused because she'd named four people plus herself, so why was it called a quad, when surely that meant four people altogether? I hung about waiting to hear what Ryan would say and got a shock when I heard his reply. "There's one name you've missed out there. And that's Sasha. But, anyway, it's early days yet. Give it time. People need to get much more practice on their own."

"I hope I don't have to go in a quad scull with Holly," I said to Izzy anxiously.

"You could tell Ryan you'd rather stay in a single," said Izzy, frowning.

"But what if I don't get a choice?"

"Don't worry about it now, Sasha. Wait till it actually happens. Ryan said give it time, didn't he? So it definitely won't be in Wednesday's session."

Izzy was right. I ought to concentrate on happy thoughts. "Guess what, Izzy?"

"What?"

"I'm so pleased that I've found something I'm quite good at..."

"*Very* good at, you mean!"

I gave Izzy a grateful smile for saying that. "And I'm determined to get as strong as I can this week by having my induction at the gym as soon as possible. Then I'll go to the gym every day and use the rowing machine, so hopefully I'll be even better next time. I'm going to try and find Mrs. Truman as soon as we get back."

"She might not be there. It's Sunday, remember," Izzy pointed out.

"But if she *is* there, just think, I could be rowing again this afternoon, and all I'll need to do is close my eyes and imagine I'm in a proper scull, not sitting on a machine!"

Izzy was frowning. "I don't think you ought to go to the gym so soon after you've been rowing though, Sasha. That might be too much for your arm muscles when you're not used to using them. I know with ballet training you have to build up your training gradually until your muscles are used to being stretched. I guess it's the same with rowing."

She's very wise, my best friend. And she was right. I would start the next day.

The others were so happy for me when Izzy and I told them all about our morning at Pollington Water. It was lunchtime and we already felt buzzy, because there's something about the grand Silver Spires dining hall and the delicious food on the menu every day that gives you a lovely warm feeling of being part of a massive family.

"Good old Sash!" said Emily, hearing our news. "You're a dark horse, aren't you!"

Antonia had been concentrating hard all the time that Izzy and I had been talking and I guessed she was trying to take in the various technical terms we used to explain everything about sculling. But her eyes shot wide open when Emily said I was a dark horse.

"It's an expression that means you've been keeping it secret that you're actually really good at something," explained Nicole.

"Except that I didn't even know I was any good at sculling until today!" I laughed.

"Not like Queen Holly!" said Izzy, lowering her voice.

The other four leaned forwards and Emily planted her elbows on the table, as Izzy told them in a low voice how good Holly was, but also how we didn't think she liked anyone else being quite as good as her.

"I can't stand show-offs," said Emily.

Bryony sighed and rolled her eyes. "She should realize that it's all about teamwork," she said simply.

"Well, she might *have* to next weekend because she's asked Ryan if she can go in a quad scull with Mikki, Charlotte, Tilly and Caitlin," said Izzy.

"A quad scull? Don't you mean a *quin* scull if it takes five altogether?" said Nicole.

"I don't think there's such a thing as a quin scull," I said, closing my eyes to get a picture of the boathouse to try and recall if there were any boats for five people in there. Come to think of it, I couldn't picture any stable quads either, and I was wondering if there even *was* such a thing. If it was a racing quad, surely it would be much too difficult for us. That made me nervous again until I remembered, with a little rush of excitement, that I was going to have a nice long chat with Mum and Dad straight after lunch, to tell them all my news. I couldn't wait.

On Monday morning I got up and dressed in tracky bums, T-shirt and trainers, packed my school uniform in my PE bag and had my school bag ready, all by quarter past seven.

"See you at breakfast!" I said to the others, as I rushed out of the dorm.

"My goodness! Someone's got the wind in their sails this morning!" said Matron, leaning over the banister as I ran downstairs.

"Going to the gym, Matron!" I called back. "Got an induction!"

"Oh! Happy induction then! Do a bit of jogging for me, won't you!"

Matron is such a friendly, jokey person. We're really lucky to have her at Forest Ash. I was smiling to myself about what she'd said as I hurried over to the sports block. I'd never heard of having the wind in your sails before, but I guessed it meant I was whizzing along really quickly. I liked that expression. If only it mentioned sculls instead of sails it would have been perfect.

The day before, I'd asked Mrs. Pridham if she thought I'd be able to book an induction at the gym, and she'd said I should ask Miss Vernon, who is actually in charge of the gym, and who should be around on a Sunday because she is the assistant housemistress at Elmhurst. I'd kept my fingers crossed as I'd run all the way to Elmhurst, but when I'd finally found my way to Miss Vernon's room I'd suddenly felt really nervous, wondering whether she'd think I was a bit cheeky coming to find her at the weekend. When I'd knocked she'd come to the door and given me a nice smile, then looked puzzled, probably because I was from a different house. But once I'd explained in a big gabble what I was there for, she'd nodded and smiled again, then invited me in to her room – which looked like more of a small flat – while she found her gym rota. I'd been so happy when I'd booked the only free spot in the whole of Monday – seven thirty in the morning.

I'd left her quite quickly, though, because I could see she was in the middle of watching something on TV, and also she looked really tired. Then I'd rushed off on cloud nine, just like I was rushing to the gym right now.

It was only seven twenty-six as I went into the sports block. I walked along the corridor, round the corner and up the stairs, my footsteps getting faster and faster, till I was right outside the gym. And then I got a horrible shock.

There was a note on the door, which said:

MISS VERNON IS UNWELL. TODAY'S INDUCTIONS ARE CANCELLED.
N.B. ON NO ACCOUNT MUST EQUIPMENT BE USED BY STUDENTS WITHOUT A MEMBER OF STAFF PRESENT.

A terrible feeling of disappointment mixed with frustration seemed to whizz round my veins as I stood there staring at the notice and remembering how Miss Vernon had been watching TV in her flat on a nice summer's afternoon and how tired she'd looked. Of course. She hadn't been well. Now I felt terrible for having disturbed her. But I also felt disappointed and let down. I couldn't help it. All my pent-up energy was collapsing.

I tried to walk away but something was rooting me to the spot and my hand couldn't help itself pushing the door open, so I could at least say I'd looked inside the gym. Maybe there were even teachers inside, so it would be okay to just pop my head around the door.

What I saw was a whole new world to me. It was a proper gym, like the one at the leisure centre where we live that Dad goes to sometimes on Sunday mornings. I stared round at the different machines and wondered what they were all for. Then I saw the rowing machine. There wasn't a teacher in sight, but I couldn't help walking towards it. I was desperate to find out how the machine worked. There was some sort of a computer on it. Maybe it could show you how fast you were going, or how far you'd rowed. Or maybe both. A little discussion between me and myself started up in my head.

Just pressing a few buttons on a machine isn't exactly using the equipment, is it?

No, that'll be fine because there's no physical danger involved. That's what you have to have the induction for, and why the member of staff has to be present – to check you're not in physical danger.

Just do it quickly. No one will ever know.

So I pressed the menu button beside the little computer screen, but absolutely nothing happened.

Of course! It wasn't plugged in.

I stared at the plug for ages, and also at the socket on the wall. To plug it in seemed like going one step further in breaking the rules. But then I reminded myself that no one would ever know, and I could unplug again the moment I'd had a look at the computer.

I picked up the plug and pushed it into its socket. At once, the little screen filled up with options. I pressed the one that said *JUST ROW*, because that was exactly what I was wishing I could do, but then there were three different screens to choose from, and I wasn't exactly sure what they all meant. One was just like a stopwatch, counting the minutes and the seconds, but the others looked as though they were showing how many metres you could travel per stroke and things like that. Until I actually started rowing I wouldn't be able to tell what they meant. But I ought to switch the machine off now and go back to the others.

I didn't though.

My mind was racing. The notice on the door made it much less likely that anyone would come in, so why didn't I just try a couple of strokes? It would be all right... Wouldn't it?

I sat down on the seat with a bit of a clunk, I was in such a hurry, and slid my feet into the foot rests, doing up the Velcro straps to make them fit tightly, so they wouldn't move when I started rowing. Then I reached for the handle and gripped it with both hands. It wasn't exactly the same as being in a scull, but it wasn't that much different. I pulled hard and it felt brilliant, especially watching the figures turn over on the little computer screen and imagining I was swishing across Pollington Water. Just a few more strokes then I'd stop.

But I'm in the swing of it now. I really want to carry on.

All the same I'd better not. It would be terrible if anyone caught me.

Okay, just one more…

"You're not supposed to use the equipment without an adult present! It says so on the door."

I turned sharply and felt my cheeks going bright red at the sound of Holly's voice right behind me.

"I…I know…I was just…"

She'd come round the side of me and was giving me a really cold look with her hands on her hips. "Anyway, I haven't seen you in here before. I bet you've not even had an induction, have you?" I shook my head, shamefully, and Holly carried on. "It's like a proper gym, you know. You have to be taught how to use the equipment. That's what Mrs. Truman says."

I swallowed, feeling really alarmed. I didn't like the way Holly had mentioned Mrs. Truman. I had an awful feeling she might report me. That would be terrible.

"I…was just trying it out to see how the computer worked. I wasn't doing it properly. Just… seeing how it worked…" My voice faded pathetically and I got off the machine and switched off the computer quickly, then switched it off at the wall as well, wondering whether Holly had had an induction herself. I noticed she was wearing cycling shorts and a skimpy top and had a towel round her neck, so she'd obviously been planning to work out. It took quite a lot of courage to ask. "Have *you* had an induction?"

"Course I have. Ages ago." She was watching me, eyebrows raised in an arch as though she couldn't believe what I'd been doing. And finally I couldn't bear her staring at me like that so I scurried out of the gym mumbling something about going to breakfast. As soon as I was in the corridor I broke into a jog, and kept it up all the way to the dining hall.

There were loos just along the corridor from the dining hall and I nipped in there to change into my uniform, then went to find my friends. It was such a relief to see Izzy and the others. There was an empty space at their table, which Izzy must have been saving for me, because she beckoned me over as I walked in, and patted the bench beside her.

"Hey! You're early. I thought you'd be much longer than this. Was it good?" she asked, as I put my cereal and toast on the table and sat down.

Emily chipped in before I had chance to answer Izzy's question. "Did you use loads of stuff or just the rower?"

"I never actually got to do anything," I said, feeling my cheeks getting hot, because I was about to admit how silly I'd been. "There was a note on the door which said that Miss Vernon was ill." I didn't add the bit about not using the equipment on any account unless a teacher was present, because my friends would think I was stupid. And they'd be right. I felt ashamed of what I'd done now, and very, very guilty. "I thought it would be okay to have the teensiest go on the rowing machine, just to see how it actually worked, because it's got its own little computer and you can see how far you've gone and how long it's taken you and everything..."

"Oh no!" said Nicole, her hand going to her mouth as though I'd done something really bad. "You didn't try it out, did you?"

This was exactly what I'd been dreading. All the way back from the gym I'd been telling myself that everything was fine and my friends would say I was being silly imagining that Holly might report me.

But already they were looking shocked and I hadn't even mentioned Holly yet.

"I...I just did a few strokes and I was about to stop..."

A little gasp came out of Antonia. "...When someone came in..." She finished off my sentence in a breathy whisper, her eyes big and round, as though she'd seen a ghost.

"Y-yes... Holly."

This time it was Izzy who gasped, but then she must have seen that she'd got me worried. "At least it wasn't a teacher," she said quickly. "Did you tell her you were just doing a few strokes, not actually using the machine properly?"

"Yes...but she kept staring at me, and saying you have to be taught how to use the equipment... and things like that..."

"Look!" hissed Emily. "She's just come into the hall."

Of course, we all looked round then and my eyes met Holly's. She was leaning forwards talking to Mikki as she stared at me with that same look in her eyes that I'd seen in the gym. Then Mikki turned round and looked at me too.

"Ignore them," said Bryony, gulping down her last mouthful of hot chocolate.

"But what if she tells Mrs. Truman?" I asked in a rush.

"Tell the truth. Say you're sorry, you know you shouldn't have done it but you thought it would be okay to see how the computer worked."

It sounded such a sensible and obvious thing to say when Bryony put it like that, but I still felt myself shuddering at the thought of having to face Mrs. Truman. Bryony and the others hadn't seen the note on the door, after all. I just had to cross my fingers and pray that Holly wouldn't tell her.

Chapter Five

I didn't enjoy the rest of that day at all because I kept on worrying about coming across Holly and wondering whether she'd told Mrs. Truman that I'd broken the gym rules. Year Sevens are divided into classes for most subjects, and sets for English, science and maths. Holly and I are only together for English, and we didn't have it that day, thank goodness.

All the same, just thinking about her made me feel guilty, and when I saw her at lunch, and later on in the corridor, I felt a big wave of worry that she'd reported me.

I could have gone to the gym after school to see if the note had been removed, but I knew it was pointless because, even if Miss Vernon had miraculously recovered, she'd already told me there wasn't another slot that day for me to have my induction. So I decided to go for a run round the athletics track. I know running isn't the same as rowing, but Mrs. Truman had stressed to us that general fitness is important in all sports, so at least it'd be doing me a bit of good.

The athletics field is huge and flat and lies near the boundary of the Silver Spires grounds. It feels very peaceful and remote, with nothing but fields stretching beyond it. You can lose yourself, as though you're in another world, when you're down there on your own. As I jogged round the track I thought back to the phone call I'd had with Mum the day before. We'd talked for ages and she'd sounded really pleased for me, but again, as I'd been talking, I'd had that feeling I so often get, that she wasn't listening properly, and that she was doing other things at the same time as talking to me. I kept on hearing her footsteps going up or down the stairs and then I'd hear her whispering something to Dad, and I had to hang on quite a few times while she popped one of the twins into a high chair or something.

"Yes, what were you saying, Sasha?" she'd say, each time she came back on the phone. But after a while I couldn't be bothered to remind her what I'd just been saying and in the end I asked if Dad was around. It took him ages to come to the phone and I think he might have been having a nap, because he sounded kind of dopey, which made me feel guilty because he works so hard all week.

He asked me straight away how the rowing had gone, and I told him it was great and I really loved it.

"We'll have to see if there's a rowing club you could go to in the summer holidays, Sash!"

"Ooh, yes! That would be brilliant!" I quickly replied.

But then after I'd rung off I wondered if Dad would remember about the rowing club or whether I'd have to remind him. I really hoped he'd be the one to bring it up, then that would prove that he was taking my big new passion seriously. Or better still, it would be great if Mum called to see how my rowing was going.

I enjoyed running round the athletics field right until the last minute when Mrs. Truman came jogging up to me just as I was about to go and get changed for supper. My heart began to pound even more than it was already after all my running. But she only said, "Well done, Sasha! Good to see someone making the effort to keep fit. It'll pay off, you'll see!"

It was the most enormous relief to realize that Holly couldn't have told her about me breaking the rules and that gave me the courage to ask, "I was supposed to be having a gym induction with Miss Vernon this morning, only she's ill. Do you know if she's better yet?"

"She's coming back to work tomorrow but I don't know if she's got any spaces for inductions."

"Shall I go and ask her?"

"No, don't disturb her now. I'll try and remember to mention it to her when I see her and she'll sort something out for you."

If only I could make Mrs. Truman understand that I actually needed to make a proper appointment as soon as I possibly could. "Erm...shall I go the gym before breakfast tomorrow so I've got a better chance of getting an induction soon?"

Mrs. Truman smiled. "Ooh, you *are* keen! Yes, try that. I can't guarantee Miss Vernon will have a space, but you never know!"

* * *

So the next day at seven thirty I jogged over to the sports hall, wearing tracksuit and trainers. Inside the building, I rushed down the corridor and up the stairs. I knew even before I'd opened the door that there were people in the gym, because I could hear the whirr of machines. Better still, the note from yesterday had been removed. Great! Miss Vernon might be able to give me my induction straight away. I could be about to get on the rowing machine! But as I walked in, my spirits sank like a stone. There were only two people in the room – an English teacher, called Miss Gardner, was running on a treadmill and Holly was on the rowing machine. The two of them were chatting away like old friends and I don't know why that made me so cross, but it did.

"Hi there! Are you okay?" asked Miss Gardner. "It's Sasha, isn't it?"

Holly turned round when she heard my name and gave me a blank look, as though she didn't know me, then whipped her head back round again.

I didn't know what to say so I just stood there feeling like a complete idiot.

"Have you had an induction, Sasha?" asked Miss Gardner.

I shook my head. "I was supposed to have one yesterday only Miss Vernon was ill."

"Miss Vernon's not here until later, but that's okay, as I'm qualified to do inductions too. I haven't got time for the full thing right now, but I can show you how the treadmills work, if you like?"

I nodded hard. This was turning out to be so much better than I'd hoped. Once Holly got off the rower I could ask about that too. Miss Gardner might not mind showing me just one more piece of equipment.

She pressed a button so her own machine came to a gradual stop, then she guided me towards one of the other treadmills and began to explain how it worked. "Okay, this is the button for a quick start. Now just start walking gently. That's right. This is the button you press to go faster or slower. Do you want to walk or run?"

"Er...run..."

"You have to remember it's set in kilometres per hour, not miles per hour, and I shouldn't go faster than eight point five to start with, just to get used to the feel of it."

Miss Gardner showed me how to slow down and stop and also how to work out how far I'd run. Then she pressed a button that made the whole treadmill move up a tiny bit, as though I was jogging on a slight slope. "If you want to make it steeper this is the button, but I wouldn't go above two if I were you. Just get used to jogging first."

She was so kind and helpful and I thanked her very much, then carried on jogging. I suddenly felt very grown up to be here in a proper gym working out before breakfast, because that's what Dad sometimes does if he's working from home, and Mum used to do it occasionally before she had the twins. I was looking forward to telling them about this in my next phone call.

Gradually I felt stronger and wished I could go faster than eight point five, but I was determined to do everything I was told from now on. That way I could make sure I didn't break any rules or ignore any advice, so I'd get fit for rowing without being too tired. It crossed my mind that I'd done lots of jogging the day before and now I was doing it again. Izzy would probably say that wasn't very good for my muscles, so I was keen to swap to the rower soon.

My eyes were continually on Holly, willing her to finish so I could have a go. Only she never did. And twenty minutes later Miss Gardner told us that we both ought to go to breakfast or we'd be late for lessons.

I felt energized from the jog, but really disappointed that I hadn't had a go on the rower. All the same, I did as I was told straight away. As I left the gym I could hear Holly telling Miss Gardner that sculling was her "thing" and she wanted to do it professionally one day. It annoyed me because it seemed like she was trying to find a reason why she ought to be allowed on the machine all the time. But she'd had one go today so it was only fair that I should have a turn after school if the machine was free, and if Miss Vernon was there to show me how to use it. I made a resolution to stand up to Holly a bit more in future, but it was a bit of a quivery resolution, because I had to remember that she could report me for breaking the rules whenever she wanted.

Some days go really slowly, and this was one of them. By the time the bell went for the end of school I was already exhausted with waiting for it. Usually Emily and Izzy are the first to shoot outside when lessons are finished, because Izzy always wants to stretch her legs after sitting still for so long, and Emily likes to breathe the fresh air after being indoors. But today, I was the first one out of my place.

I got changed in the PE changing room and raced upstairs, looking forward to that moment when I was close enough to the gym to hear the whirring of machinery. Yes! It sounded like lots of machines were in use this time. I crossed my fingers that the rower might be available and, more importantly, that Miss Vernon might be there.

And when I went in I was immediately hit by the difference in the atmosphere at this time of day. The place was full of older students and a few teachers. My eyes went straight to the rowing machine and a whoosh of happiness zipped through me. It was free. Then I got another jolt of happiness, because Miss Vernon had spotted me and was coming over looking apologetic.

"Sorry, Sasha! I was really under the weather yesterday. And sorry again, because I can't fit you in today either." She was reaching for her rota. "Looks like I could manage—"

But I interrupted her. "Miss Gardner taught me how to use the treadmill but all I really want to learn to use is the rowing machine." I pointed to it, feeling a sudden sense of urgency to get on it before anyone else did, because people were moving from one piece of equipment to another all the time.

Miss Vernon looked at her watch, then nodded.

"Okay, I've got time to show you that, no problem."

I hurried over to it but it was only once I was sitting astride the machine with my feet strapped into the metal "shoes" on the sides and my hands holding the T-shaped handle that I relaxed and started to enjoy myself.

Miss Vernon pressed the menu on the computer and a couple of other buttons. She showed me which figures indicated the distance I was covering, and how fast I was going, and how many strokes per minute I was taking. Then there was a large figure in the left-hand corner which showed the seconds ticking away. I pulled hard over and over again and Miss Vernon told me to use my legs more and my back. I loved the feeling I got when my strokes per minute score went up. But the best feeling was when she said she thought I was a natural rower. Then she told me I could keep going, but not for more than ten minutes, and to let her know if I had any problems.

The following day was Wednesday. I could hardly wait for the sculling session that evening. But I was up bright and early again, determined to have just a short warm-up session on the rowing machine before breakfast, so long as my muscles could take it. As soon as I'd jumped out of bed I started swinging my arms around to check they didn't feel stiff. They felt fine, so that was my decision made.

"You've really got the bug, haven't you?" said Emily, when she saw me rushing off before breakfast again.

"Good luck, Sash!" Izzy called after me. "I'll save you a place at breakfast."

I was early. It was only seven twenty-six by my watch when I went into the sports block, so I guessed I'd have to wait until seven thirty, but I didn't care. At least I'd be first in, and I couldn't help hoping that Holly wouldn't show up.

It gave me a bit of a shock to hear the unmistakable sound of machinery whirring as I pushed the door open, and an even bigger shock to see Holly on the rowing machine, and Miss Gardner on one of the treadmills. It was still only seven twenty-eight so Holly must have started before she was supposed to, but then I supposed that if Miss Gardener had said it was okay, she wasn't breaking the rules or anything.

"All right?" Miss Gardner asked me, panting a bit and throwing me a smile.

If I'd answered her truthfully I would have said,

No, I am not all right, and why has Holly been allowed to start before half past seven? but I just mumbled, "Fine, thanks," and went onto one of the treadmills.

I waited twenty minutes for Holly to get off the rowing machine so I could have a go, but she never did and in the end I went off to breakfast, feeling frustrated and cross.

"Never mind," said Izzy, when I told her. "You'll be doing the real thing in..." She glanced at her watch, then frowned. "In...erm..."

"Nine hours," said Nicole.

I smiled inside at that, and tried to ignore the little shiver that ran through me at the thought that I might have to be in the same scull as Holly and some of her friends.

As it happened, I didn't have to worry about that at all. The second session at Pollington Water was even better than the first. Ryan told us right at the beginning that he just wanted us to consolidate what we'd learned during our first session and gain confidence in the single sculls. Some people, who were struggling, had to stay on ropes for quite a while, but several of us were allowed to go off on our own straight away.

George marked out various routes with buoys of different colours and told everyone which route they should use. Holly and I were allowed to go further than anyone else, but there was always at least one of the coaches keeping an eye on us. At first it was easy to keep my distance from Holly because, when we were told we could set off, she pulled away really quickly.

"Good work, Holly!" called Ryan.

"I've been in the gym," Holly answered. "I'm going to see how often I can do the circuit George has marked out before the end of the session."

"Excellent!" said Ryan. "But don't overdo it – and I mean that, Holly. You're not used to sculling yet."

"Yes I am. I've done it loads – remember, I told you!" she called back, grinning at him.

He grinned back but didn't say anything.

I took my time and then set off slowly so that there wasn't any chance that I'd catch her up. Half of me actually felt the urge to go racing after her. It would be such a challenge to catch her up, but the other half couldn't bear the thought that she might be all hostile again.

I felt like singing as I rowed this time and after a while I did actually start humming to myself. It was hard work, though, and I think my arms and legs might have been suffering slightly after the sessions at the gym, so I couldn't help wondering what Holly's arms felt like.

The water seemed darker today, probably because it was a different time of day. And the sky was a beautiful, heavy blue colour that blended somehow with my blades as they cut through the water. It was as though I was in tune with every single thing around me. I'd never felt anything like it before.

The circuit took me almost to the island and as I turned to row back towards the lakeside, I could see the sailing boats in the distance more clearly. Then the nearer I got to the lakeside again, the more I had to concentrate, because this patch of water was full of boats and I didn't want to crash into anyone. It was a relief when I turned again and headed back to the peace of the water near the island.

Much later, when I was on my third lap, I realized that Holly was catching up with me. That meant she was on her fourth lap, which was amazing. Every so often she glanced round to check where she was going, but she never actually looked straight at me, which made me feel awkward again. It was a shame she didn't seem to like me, because she obviously loved rowing as much as I did and I thought how great it would be to have someone to talk to about it.

Eventually she overtook me and I impulsively called, "Wow! You're doing really well, Holly!" She did a kind of grunt which might have been "Thanks", but I couldn't really tell.

I didn't mind when the session came to an end this time, because I was tired and happy. Celia had helped me to get better at turning the boat neatly and backing it down, and she'd explained how important it was not to tire myself out with short hard strokes, but to ease off with longer slower ones sometimes. I had such a feeling of satisfaction that I went straight over to Izzy afterwards to talk about it. She was happy too because she'd been on her own for the last part of the session and managed without the rope.

"Okay," said Ryan, calling us all to attention. "Great work from you all today. I think every single one of you has made progress. Now, on Saturday afternoon when you come, I'm going to set up a quad scull. I'd like Holly, Sasha, Mikki, Charlotte and Tilly to try working in the quad as a team. The quads that we've got here are nice and wide, so you'll feel very stable. Four of you will be sculling and the fifth will be cox. If you're cox you have to make sure you're really bossy!" We all laughed. "No, seriously, a good cox has to be able to shout out instructions to the team so that they work together in the best possible way. Anyway, I won't go into that now, but you five will hopefully all get a chance to try being cox. And actually, every one of you is doing so well –" Ryan smiled round at all of us – "that there might be a few more of you ready for a quad either later on Saturday or in the following session. "

My spirits were sinking fast. I couldn't imagine anyone taking instructions from me. It was a real worry. But then I tried to snap myself out of it. Really, it was only Holly who I didn't think would take instructions from me. And I was cross with myself for letting her get to me so much. Once, at primary school, when I was scared of an older girl who was always teasing me, Mum had told me I should grow a thicker skin. I can remember her exact words. "You need a nice thick skin, then no one can touch you, darling!"

I was sure that was good advice. But getting out of the minibus when we got back to Silver Spires, and watching Holly's hair swing from side to side as she waltzed along, it seemed to me that growing a thicker skin was going to be easier said than done.

Chapter Six

The next two days whizzed by and on Saturday afternoon, the sun was shining brightly again and my whole body felt alive at the thought that we were off to the lake. I'd managed one more turn on the rowing machine on Thursday lunchtime but not at all on Friday, because Holly was always on it. I wasn't so worried about having to be in a quad scull with her now, though, because all my friends had convinced me that I shouldn't let myself be forced into anything I didn't want to do.

"Just tell Ryan you're happier on your own," Emily had reminded me firmly before she'd gone off to the stables. "Don't even think about going in with Holly if you don't want to, okay!"

So, as the minibus drew up in the car park at Pollington Water I was all ready to tell Ryan that I'd prefer to stick with a single scull if that was all right.

"Anyway, you never know, he might have completely forgotten about wanting you to go in a quad!" said Izzy, as we went to the boathouse to help carry the boats down to the water.

But there was no chance of that.

"Don't worry, girls!" was the first thing Ryan said. "Ben and I have already got the quad scull down there, so you've managed to escape the hardest work!"

"Er...excuse me, Ryan," I began quietly, once we were outside the boathouse and no one else but Izzy could hear what I was saying, "would it be okay for me to stay in a single scull instead of going in the quad?"

"What?" he said, pretending to be horrified. "No way! I want my students making progress not standing still! Keeping in time with other rowers is the next step, and you're someone with big potential, Sasha! You'll enjoy it, you know! It's a great feeling when you're part of a team all managing to keep together!"

So I just had to accept it. Izzy gave me a sympathetic smile as she stepped into a single with Celia's help. I so envied Izzy at that moment but I was trying to hang on to what Ryan had said. Maybe I *would* enjoy it more than I thought. Maybe Holly would forget about being competitive with me once there were three other girls in the boat, but that seemed a little unlikely.

To start with we had to go to a room in the clubhouse where there was a rowing machine.

"Okay, girls," Ryan began, when the five of us were gathered around him. "Now, as I started to explain at the end of the last session, the cox is the person who gives instructions to the rowers. She sits in the stern of the boat. And because she can see ahead and the scullers can't, it's the cox's job to keep the crew rowing in time with each other, to steer them, and generally to encourage them. So let's get used to that before we go down and try it for real."

While we each took turns on the rowing machine, Ryan called out instructions as though he was the cox, then we all had a go at giving the commands. Because there was so much to remember, and I was concentrating as hard as I could, I didn't have time to think about Holly. The only slightly awkward moment was when it was her turn on the machine and I had to shout commands to her. I couldn't bring myself to shout, and Ryan said I had to be more assertive. I noticed as she got off the machine she exchanged a look with Mikki, which made me feel a bit hurt, because it was obvious the others saw it too.

After we got the hang of the basics Ryan explained that, if we were in a race, we'd have to start off with shorter strokes to get the boat moving. The technical names for them are "half" and "three quarters", and they tell us how long a stroke to take. Then we'd change to longer strokes, which is called "striding", otherwise we'd get exhausted.

Ryan led us down to the landing stage, where the quad was waiting for us.

"This is where the cox sits. You'll notice it's much lower down than the rowers' seats. Now, in a quad scull, the cox steers by moving these toggles." Ryan held one in each hand and showed us how the wires attached to them made the rudder turn, which turned the boat. This seat here –" Ryan pointed to the seat nearest to the cox's seat – "is the number four position, and it's generally the strongest and most rhythmical rower who takes this place. Another name for number four is stroke. Then there are positions three and two, and lastly the rower sitting at the front of the boat, who is furthest away from the cox, is number one or bow, same as the name of the front of the boat. You don't have to be such a strong oarswoman to row at bow," Ryan was saying, "but you should be nice and accurate and keep it level."

"You ought to be bow, Sasha," Holly suddenly said. "And I'll be stroke as I'm probably the strongest, aren't I?" She was looking at the other girls with her eyebrows raised.

They all nodded, but Charlotte said, "I don't mind which position I'm in."

"You can keep swapping round," said Ryan, "so you all get a go in every position. I'll cox first..." He looked round the five of us. "Tilly, do you mind just watching from here for a few minutes while I demonstrate the kind of thing we've just been practising with the rowing machine?"

Tilly said she didn't mind at all, so we put the blades in and got in the boat carefully. Mikki was in the bow position, at the front of the boat, but behind the other rowers. Then I was in front of her at number two, Holly was in front of me, and finally Charlotte was facing Ryan, at stroke. Ryan sat in the cox's seat and told each of us to shout out our position – "Bow" and "Two" and so on – once we'd got our gates done up and were ready.

"Now this is more difficult than single sculling, because you really have to work together and keep to the same rhythm, otherwise the oars will get all tangled up. Try not to look at your own oars, but keep watching stroke's."

After that Ryan called, "Whole crew come forward and square up!" He'd already told us that this meant we had to bend our legs, as we'd practised in the Viruses, and put our arms straight out, then make sure our blades were buried in the water, ready to row. "This is the 'catch' position," Ryan explained. Next he told us to sit up tall, keep relaxed and start sculling when he gave the command. "Whole crew, paddling light, are you ready...? Go!"

And off we went. Once we were properly in the rhythm and going well he said, "Sit up and drive *now*! Legs *now*! Drive *now*!"

It was hard work and you had to concentrate like mad, but I absolutely loved it. Working in a team and being exactly in time with the others was the best feeling ever. And it was so brilliant to feel how much faster we could move along through the water with four of us rowing instead of just me. I didn't even mind that I was right behind Holly, because

I hardly gave it a thought and, anyway, Ryan was there.

After a few minutes, Tilly, who'd been watching and listening from the side, swapped places with Ryan, and the rest of us stayed in the same positions. I'd have been really nervous if I'd been Tilly, so I wasn't really surprised that she kept breaking into nervous giggles when she first started directing us, as though she found it a bit embarrassing. But Holly told her off.

"Be serious, Tilly. It's an important role. Do you want me to do it?"

"I'll just try for a bit longer, then you can take over," Tilly replied. But she couldn't really remember what she had to say and a few minutes later we went back to the landing stage, where Ryan supervised us as we swapped over.

"Move round, girls," he said. "Let's try Sasha as stroke."

This was exactly what I'd been dreading. It meant I had to be directly facing Holly while she gave the instructions.

"Are you okay?" mouthed Izzy from her scull just nearby, when she saw where I was sitting.

I nodded and tried to smile, because I didn't want Izzy to worry about me. I thought she had enough anxieties with the actual rowing. But then I had a nice surprise because she gave me a big grin.

"Look! I can turn the scull round now!"

I didn't have time to watch so I just called out, "Hey! Well done, Iz!" and thought about how great it would be if I could be in a double scull with Izzy. Maybe I'd ask Ryan about that.

As soon as we set off, with Holly coxing, I felt myself tensing up and knew I wasn't sculling as well as before. She remembered all the commands and yelled them out as though we were deaf, but Ryan praised her and said, "That's right. Take control, Holly. Show them who's in charge!" Then he said he was going off to see how everyone else was getting on, and he'd be back shortly.

The moment he'd gone, Holly suddenly seemed to work us even harder. Her commands were getting faster and louder and she didn't let up at all. "*Now!* Legs *now*! Drive *now*! Legs *now*!" We were heading towards the island and I found myself struggling to keep up with the speed and wondered if it was my fault for overdoing it on the rowing machine during the week. I wished I knew if the others also felt as though their arms and legs would drop off, but I was determined to keep going, because it would be so humiliating if Holly thought I wasn't strong enough to be stroke, and said something to embarrass me in front of the others.

After a minute or two though, I realized that our oars were getting in a tangle, which meant that one of the others, or maybe more than one, hadn't been able to keep up with the speed, which wasn't surprising.

"Oh, guys! You've lost it!" said Holly, sitting up straight and pursing her lips, then shrugging dramatically as though we were hopeless.

It wasn't our fault, it was hers, and I wished I had the nerve to say so, but I didn't. We just weren't experienced or fit enough to scull as fast as she was trying to make us do it.

"What are you trying to do, kill us?" said Charlotte. "Wait till it's my turn to cox, then I'll show you what it's like."

When I turned round to look at Mikki and Tilly they seemed too exhausted to speak, but they were both nodding and rolling their eyes.

"The trouble was, Sasha lost the speed," said Holly, not looking at me. "It's up to stroke to lead the others, so that's why you got in a mess."

And then I saw that Ryan was right beside us and at the same time I felt my face flooding with colour. "How's it going?" he asked. "Looked like you were doing brilliantly when I was watching you just then."

"Holly was making us go too fast," puffed Charlotte.

"We couldn't keep up," said Tilly. "Can someone else be cox now?"

"Ready for another change around?" said Ryan. "Okay, come back in, then try Sasha as cox and you go at stroke, Holly."

My heart sank. This was going to be worse than ever. Ryan stayed alongside as we rowed back to the landing stage and it made me cross that Holly was on her best behaviour, coxing in a loud, encouraging voice and sticking to a much steadier speed so we could all manage to keep in time with each other.

As we changed places I looked round for Izzy and saw that she was in a quad scull with Penny coxing. It wasn't going very well because the boat was weaving about all over the place and the oars seemed to be in loads of different positions. I could hear Penny calling out instructions but the girls didn't look anxious or anything. In fact Izzy seemed to have broken into giggles with the girl behind her, and I thought how much more fun she was having than me.

"Okay, Sasha, do your stuff!" said Ryan. "Don't be afraid to be bossy!"

I tried to smile at him but I think it must have come out looking a bit lopsided because I was remembering that look that Holly and Mikki had exchanged when we were practising on the rowing machine. Then when we set off my mind went blank. I was racking my brains to try to remember what Ryan had said, but it was no good, I'd forgotten, and he'd already gone off to help some others leaving only Ben near us. I couldn't ask Ben what to say because I'd feel such an idiot. I had to say something though, so I tried to imagine that I was one of the rowers. What would I want to hear?

For a start I wouldn't want someone yelling at me so much. I'd want to feel relaxed. That's right. Ryan had started off by telling us to sit up and relax.

"Sit up and relax everyone," I began. And as soon as those words were out of my mouth, I just seemed to know what to say next, and in no time at all they were all pulling really well.

"Well done, Sasha!" called Ben, drawing nearer.

Holly had been wearing the same expression, her eyes dull and staring at a point way behind me, ever since I'd been cox. But when Ben spoke, she suddenly seemed to come alive. "We can go much faster than this, you know!"

"Better to take it steady and keep together," said Ben, which pleased me. But still Holly's words had made me lose a bit of confidence. What if she wasn't the only one who wanted to go faster? No, I was sure the others liked this speed – after all, they'd said that Holly had made us go too fast. But even as I was thinking these thoughts I realized I was losing concentration. And then I lost more confidence as Mikki called out, "Speak up, Sasha! I can't hear you."

I tried my best. I really did, but it obviously didn't work, because after only a few seconds everyone's oars were out of time with each other and Holly looked totally hacked off. She turned round to Mikki, who was behind her and said something that I couldn't hear, then Mikki said, "Yeah, okay."

"Mikki's going to be cox now," Holly told me. And I felt cross that she'd made that decision herself, as though she was one of the coaches. But I didn't have the confidence to question her, so I just nodded.

"Okay."

"It's not fair!" said Emily, putting her arm around me. "Holly's spoiling the course for you, isn't she, Sash?"

I nodded miserably.

The six of us were all crammed onto my bed in our dorm, because I'd called a truth talk. That's a meeting we have when someone in the group isn't happy about something and needs the support of her friends. This time it was my turn, and already I was feeling better. Less alone. It was Antonia who'd thought of calling these meetings "truth talks", in the first term here at Silver Spires, when her English wasn't so good. We all loved the name she'd come up with, so we'd kept using it, and now it had stuck.

"I saw you having fun in your boat, Iz, and I just wished I could have been with you instead of having to put up with Holly."

"Well, actually, we've got a bit of a 'Holly' in our boat too," said Izzy, looking thoughtful for a moment. "Caitlin."

"Really? Caitlin?" Izzy had surprised me, because I thought her team was getting on so well together.

"She's probably nowhere near as bad as Holly," Izzy explained, "but she thinks she's better than the rest of us. First she criticized Laura's coxing, then she criticized the rest of us for not keeping in time. And *then*, when we were packing up, I heard her asking Ryan if she could go in your boat, Sash, next time."

"What did Ryan say?"

"I didn't hear."

"Sounds like the perfect solution would be for you and Caitlin to swap with each other," said Bryony in her usual straightforward way.

"Sasha won't want to join our team," said Izzy, shaking her head as though it was out of the question. "You're way better than us lot, Sash," she went on. "We all row miles more slowly than your team, and we keep getting it wrong too."

But I was feeling a new excitement mounting inside me. What a brilliant challenge it would be to try and help Izzy's team to build confidence and do well. And how different it would be to have Izzy's lovely smiley face in front of me instead of Holly's mean face.

"You know, I think you've got a really good idea there, Bryony," I told her slowly. Then I turned to Izzy. "I'd love to swap with Caitlin. It'd be great to cox for your team. I actually enjoyed that role, apart from having to put up with Holly, of course. And Ben said I was doing well."

"Penny said you were doing well, too!" said Izzy. "She made us all stop and watch your team when you were cox, and she said you were leading perfectly, because the scull was going along so smoothly. I felt really proud of you!"

I gave Izzy a hug for saying that. "Let's ask Caitlin tomorrow if she wants to swap."

"But are you *sure*, Sash?"

I actually felt more sure of this than anything since I'd started the rowing course. "Totally!"

"That's settled then!" said Emily. "I declare this meeting closed!"

"It was Sasha who asked for the truth talk!" said Antonia, sticking to the rules. "So Sasha has to say when it's finished."

I smiled at her. "Okay, *I* now declare this meeting closed!"

And everyone laughed.

Chapter Seven

As soon as we were on the minibus on our way to Pollington Water the next day, I started to worry.

"What if Caitlin agrees to swap with me but Ryan says we're not allowed?" I whispered to Izzy in what she calls my quivery voice.

"We'll beg!" said Izzy. She was smiling confidently, as though she knew that begging wouldn't really be necessary. But I wasn't so sure.

I was dreading Ryan saying no, because I'd got it in my head I was going to be with Izzy. And it would be such a disappointment if I had to go back with Holly after all.

"Do you want to talk to Caitlin or shall I?" said Izzy.

I said I'd do it myself, so she'd see I was really keen on the swap, and as she was right in front of me I decided to get it over with straight away. If she said yes, it would feel like I'd won half the battle – well, maybe about a third of the battle.

"Hey, cool!" was what she actually said. But she looked totally happy. "Are you sure? Your team's much better than mine, you know." She was raising her eyebrows to check I really meant it, but she didn't give me time to answer. "Oh, is it so you and Izzy can be together?"

It seemed simplest just to say yes, so I did.

"That's a good omen," whispered Izzy, when Caitlin had turned back to the front. "Now just Ryan to get round."

Once we'd got off the minibus, I kept putting off speaking to Ryan, because I was so dreading what he would say. Caitlin must have been assuming he would easily agree, though, because I'd already heard her gleefully telling Charlotte and Holly that she was swapping places with me. I'd watched

Holly's face carefully at that moment, expecting her to break into a big smile of relief that she'd finally got rid of me, but she just shrugged as though she didn't really care either way, and I was puzzled for a moment. I *had* got Holly right, hadn't I?

"You'd better say something to Ryan, Sash," said Izzy, beginning to look anxious, as we walked down to the landing stage. So I took the chance to run over to Caitlin while she was on her own, and ask her if she wanted to come with me to check it was okay with Ryan if we swapped.

"Yeah, sure!" she said. And off we went together.

It only took Ryan a few seconds of what Emily would call deep-frowning-thinking before he nodded. "If you're sure that's what you want."

Caitlin and I both thanked him, then ran off happily. Well, at least Caitlin was happy, because she started shouting across to Charlotte that she was coming to join her in the top team, as she called it. And I was happy too, but not so I felt like shouting about it. I was pleased that I'd be with Izzy and wouldn't have to suffer Holly any more, but there was still a small part of me wondering if I should have done what Mum used to talk about, and grown a thicker skin.

I decided that the best way to work with my new

team was to be very patient, because it was obvious they were much more jittery than my other team. They couldn't really scull in time with each other at all. Penny was close by in a little inflatable dinghy, though, and she started calling out instructions. But I wished she wouldn't, because I wanted to cox on my own. It was quite a relief when Ryan asked her to come and help him.

"Just keep it steady!" she called over her shoulder as she zoomed off. "George and Ben are both around if you need them."

"Oh, we're useless!" said Laura straight away. She pointed to Holly's team, who were already a long way from the landing stage, heading out to the island with Tilly coxing and Holly at stroke.

A little pang of disappointment that I wasn't part of that team, slicing through the water like that, went through me. But I quickly shook it away and concentrated on the challenge of my own team.

"You're not useless. You're good. We'll soon be out there just like them."

Robyn, the girl who was sitting at stroke, suddenly shivered, and I realized they all looked cold, so I knew I must set to work quickly. I gave myself a firm talking to. *Just take charge properly, Sasha. Act like Ryan or one of the other coaches.*

"Okay, sit at backstops and turn the oars so that the spoon is square," I began. "And get ready to push your hands down...now!" Amazingly they did it exactly together and I felt my first little thrill of pride. "Straighten your arms, that's right...now lift your hands...and pull right to your stomach... and push down..." They were still completely in time. I had to keep my voice loud and firm. That was the secret. "Lift and...pull...and push...and lift and pull..."

I kept repeating the instructions at the top of my voice to make sure that Sabrina could hear me right from the bow position and also to encourage everyone. Gradually I realized they were actually sculling along quite smoothly.

"Hey! We're doing okay!" called Laura, with laughter in her voice.

"You're such a good cox, Sasha!" yelled Sabrina from the back.

"Don't talk or you'll..."

And, of course, the moment I broke off giving them my instructions, they lost the rhythm.

"Sorry, that was my fault," I said, feeling cross with myself for falling into such an obvious trap.

I started them off from scratch again and this time nobody talked. Everyone concentrated on rowing, and though we were nowhere near as good as Holly's team, I felt as though we were definitely improving. And I realized something else, too. I was really enjoying myself.

"Good teamwork!" said Ryan, passing us at one point. "Do you want to swap positions?"

"No chance!" said Sabrina. "No one else could cox like Sasha!"

Ryan nodded, then fixed me with that same careful look that he'd used before. "What about you, Sasha? Did you want to scull for a while?"

I only hesitated for a second, because there was still a part of me that wished I was actually sculling, but the much bigger part was filled with determination to get my team as good as Holly's. Well, maybe that was a bit too ambitious, but I thought we could still make loads more improvement.

"No, I'm fine," I told him firmly.

"Great! Keep up the good work then!"

And that's what we did. I worked the team quite hard, but they didn't seem to mind at all. We just kept practising going in a straight line and keeping in time with each other, and by the time the session was over, I felt really pleased with the improvement our team had made.

"Right," said Ryan, gathering us together when the session was over, "you've all done brilliantly to make the amount of progress you've made at this stage of the course. Hopefully, by the end of next Saturday's session, we'll have the last five girls working together in a quad too. Then on the Sunday we can have a three-boat race."

"But the other two teams are way better than us!" wailed Poppy instantly. She was one of the ones who hadn't been formed into a quad team yet. "There's no way we can win if we have a race!"

"Yes," agreed Poppy's friend, Ali. "We don't stand a chance!"

"Hold on! Hold on!" said Ryan. I glanced over at Holly and saw that she was standing with her head on one side, looking at Ryan, waiting to hear what he said. "We can stagger the three boats so that you don't all set off at the same time, then it'll be perfectly fair."

"Oh right, so you mean Poppy's scull will set off first, then Sasha's, then ours?" said Holly, smiling at Ryan.

"Yes..." said Ryan, nodding slowly as though he was still thinking about it. "Something like that."

Holly turned slowly to smile at Mikki as Ryan clapped his hands. "Okay, that's all I wanted to say.

Have a good week, girls, and see you next Saturday afternoon. We won't have the race till Sunday, but remember to keep up your general fitness. That's the secret with any sport."

Yes, I thought happily, I *will* keep up my fitness, and I'll make sure I encourage my team to go to the gym too. But more than that, I planned to talk to Dad as soon as possible about carrying on sculling in the summer holidays. I loved my new sport and I wasn't going to let it out of my life. Not ever.

Chapter Eight

I was in the dining hall eating pudding with my friends the next day when Sabrina and Robyn came up to me with faces like thunder. They both started gabbling at once.

"We've had our inductions at the gym but it's impossible to get on the rowing machine. Holly's always hogging it."

"Robyn tried before breakfast," said Sabrina, "and I tried just now."

I knew how they felt but I had absolutely no idea what to suggest.

"If Holly's on it now, then there'll still be time for

you to have a go before afternoon lessons," said Nicole. "She's not going to keep rowing for all that time is she?"

"Is there a teacher in there?" I asked.

"Miss Fosbrook."

Izzy turned to me with her shoulders slumped. "Remember I said I'd go after school? Well, now I'm thinking it's not worth bothering."

"Sounds like you need to see Mrs. Truman," said Bryony in her usual matter-of-fact way. Then she gulped the last bit of water in her tumbler. "She'll sort out a rota to make it fair. Why don't you go and find her right now?"

That's what I so admire about Bryony. She doesn't waste words and she doesn't waste time.

"Hey, good plan!" said Sabrina.

And Izzy and I exchanged a hopeful smile.

"Right, Holly, can you just stop a moment please."

Holly turned round mid-stroke, and looked shocked to hear Mrs. Truman's voice. Then immediately her expression turned cold and cross as she saw me, with Sabrina, Robyn, Laura and Izzy, coming into the gym behind Mrs. Truman. She stopped rowing but kept her back to us. Miss

Fosbrook was on the treadmill wearing earphones. She scarcely gave us a glance.

I wondered if Mrs. Truman might think Holly was a bit rude, but she didn't seem to notice. She was scribbling on her clipboard in a big hurry. I think she just wanted to sort things out as quickly as possible. It was amazing that she'd agreed with us straight away about the rower, when we'd explained how we all wanted to train but no one was getting the chance. And she'd told us to come with her to the gym right then and there.

"It's great that you're all so keen to get fit," she said now. "And I'm only sorry we don't have more than one rowing machine. Now, Holly, I think you've been the lucky one till now, so I'm going to try to make it a bit fairer."

Holly glanced up. She flashed me that same cold look again, and immediately I felt my heart thudding at the thought that she might tell Mrs. Truman how I'd broken the rules the week before.

Mrs. Truman was frowning at her clipboard. "We need to get a rota sorted for this rower, as it's proving so popular, otherwise some girls won't get a look in. I think I'll have a word with a few of the teachers who like to use the gym, and I'm sure they won't mind sorting out a rota for themselves, so that there'll always be an adult here. Now, at the moment, there are six of you wanting to use the machine—"

"Why does Sasha need to have a go?" interrupted Holly, looking sulky. "She's not even a rower. She's the cox."

My heart started beating faster. Why was Holly being so mean?

Mrs. Truman sounded a bit irritated when she answered Holly. "That's entirely up to Sasha." But then Mrs. Truman turned to me, and raised her eyebrows in a question.

"I...still want to keep fit..." I said in a murmur.

"And what about the rest of *my* team?" Holly went on, in a very clipped voice. "They all want a go."

I wished I had the courage to point out that none of Holly's team had shown the slightest interest so far, and that it looked like Holly was just making things as awkward as possible for my team. But of course I didn't dare say anything like that.

Only then it turned out that Sabrina must have been thinking exactly the same thing as me. "So how come the rest of your team hasn't been anywhere near the gym?" she asked.

Holly leaped off the rowing machine looking really angry, but Mrs. Truman put a hand up to stop her replying. "I'm not wasting my time listening to you lot arguing," she said crossly. "Work out how many people want to use the rower and tell me their names by the end of afternoon lessons, then I'll put a rota up on the sports noticeboard, and hopefully the problem will be sorted."

On Wednesday I talked to Mum on the phone. Sometimes I e-mail her and Dad because then I can be sure that Mum will be paying attention to my news, instead of half listening to me and half dealing with the twins. I'd already sent her an e-mail explaining a bit about the weekend, but now I felt like having a proper conversation. I wanted to tell her all that had been happening *since* the weekend too. So I texted first to ask her to phone me when it was convenient, and she phoned back almost immediately, which was a nice surprise.

I walked round the grounds as I talked to her, as it was such a nice day.

"Have you just finished lessons, Sash?" she asked me first.

"Yes and Izzy's gone to the gym. You know I told you about that girl Holly who kind of took over the rowing machine last week, so I hardly got a go?"

"Uh-huh," said Mum, though it didn't sound like she remembered.

I tried not to let that put me off. "Well, this week it started happening all over again, only now there's my whole sculling team, not just me, wanting to go on it. And Holly said *her* sculling team wanted to use it as well—"

Mum suddenly laughed. "Slow down, Sasha! I can't keep up. So there are loads of people all wanting to use just the one rowing machine. Is that it?"

"Yes, and Mrs. Truman has organized a rota now, so it's much fairer…"

"Oh good."

"But Holly's not very happy about me being on the rota because she doesn't think coxes ought to have a turn, as they don't have to do any actual rowing. But I stuck up for myself for once."

I waited for Mum to praise me and say that was good, but instead she asked me another question and I could hear the confusion in her voice.

"So why *did* you want to be on the rota?"

"Because…I still love rowing," I told Mum in answer to her question. "And, basically, I want to get fit and strong."

"Oh, right," said Mum, sounding a bit surprised.

"Well there's nothing wrong with that."

"Yes, but Holly's really cross. I mean she's never been exactly friendly with me, but it's worse than that. She doesn't talk to me at all, doesn't even look at me. It's horrible when someone treats you like that."

"Yes, I know it is, Sash," said Mum, full of sympathy now, which made me suddenly feel close to tears, because she seemed to have properly understood why I was upset. "But you just have to remember that it's not your problem, it's Holly's. And only *she* can sort it out. Just act as normally as you can towards her. There's nothing more you can do than that, I'm afraid, love."

Mum made it all sound so easy, and I wished, for the hundredth time, that I was more thick-skinned, but I wasn't. It was as simple as that. I sighed and went back to talking about the weekend. I really wanted Mum to realize that Ryan thought I was doing really well, so then she'd be proud of me.

"It was great when I managed to get the new team all sculling in time with each other, Mum!" I told her, trying to get my own excitement to magically travel down the phone line.

"Well done! You clever thing!" she said brightly.

I should have been pleased, because her actual

words were a compliment, but somehow, the way Mum had said them, they just didn't sound right. I couldn't work out why at first, but a moment later I heard one of the twins crying and realized that Mum must have heard it long before I did, and she'd stopped paying attention to what I was saying, and started concentrating on them instead. As usual.

As I rang off I couldn't help feeling disappointed. I wanted Mum to be properly proud of me. Not just proud in words.

Most of my nervousness fizzled away once Saturday afternoon arrived. We were all standing on the side of the lake, putting on our buoyancy aids, ready to get in our boats, and I just felt a lovely excitement that I was about to be working with my team.

In the distance, I could see two older boys in a racing double. I couldn't stop watching the way their blades seemed to cut through the water so perfectly as they zoomed along smoothly and really quickly.

"I love coxing, but I love sculling too," I said with a sigh to Izzy, who was standing next to me on the landing stage. "I wish I could do both!"

"No reason why you shouldn't!" came Ryan's voice from behind me.

I hadn't realized he was so near.

"Right, this is the plan for the start of today's session," he went on, raising his voice to talk to the whole group. "If you want to break up the quads and go back to single sculls for a while, that's fine, or if all five in a quad are happy to stick with that, then that's fine too. Let's have single scullers over there and quads over here."

I suddenly felt like a bit of a traitor to my team, but good old Izzy quickly explained to them that I wanted to scull on my own for a bit, and they all agreed that was perfectly fair.

"But you will come back to us afterwards, won't you?" said Laura, looking worried.

"Course I will!" I assured her.

Sculling on my own felt wonderful. I noticed that Holly's quad had decided to stay together but I made sure I was sculling as far away from them as possible. Celia came alongside me for quite a while and gave me a lovely compliment, which made me so happy.

"You know, if I'd only just come across you now, I'd think you'd been sculling for months! Really good work, Sasha!"

I smiled at her and tried not to look show-offy.

Then her voice went quieter. "When you go back to the quad, if you'd like to change to sculling, rather than coxing, that's not a problem, you know."

"No, it's fine. I do like coxing," I said, looking forward to it again now I'd had some time on my own.

So about half an hour later we all had a change around and everyone went in a quad scull, even the five who'd never done it before. Penny and Ryan were coaching that third team and Celia was with my team. I could see George with Holly's team and guessed he was working with them.

"Okay, Sasha," said Celia, "when you're ready, tell your team to number off from bow."

I gave the command to my team and they answered straight away, as though I was calling the register.

"Bow!" said Laura. "Two!" came Izzy's voice, then "Three!" said Robyn, and lastly from Sabrina, "Stroke!"

"Well done!" said Celia. "Now let me hear you get them started, Sasha."

Everyone in my team was perfectly silent when we set off. It was great that they were all taking it so seriously. The rota for the rowing machine had worked really well, and my team now looked fit and strong. Plus they were all raring to go. I kept my voice loud and tried to be as encouraging as possible, and after a while I could feel that we were getting faster.

"Big improvement! Bravo!" called out George, who was the nearest coach to us at that moment.

None of us looked round or replied, we just kept working... "Long and strong!" I called. "Relax and drive! Well done, team!" And I suddenly felt so proud of them.

Izzy said afterwards that it had felt as though we'd all been working together for weeks. I remembered Celia's compliment from earlier on, and felt brilliant.

On Saturday evening, Izzy and I couldn't talk about anything except sculling, and the others kept on saying things like, "It's not fair! Why can't we come and watch the race tomorrow? We could cheer you on!"

In the end we went down to Mrs. Pridham's flat and asked her if it would be possible for Emily, Bryony, Nicole and Antonia to come along to Pollington Water with us the next day.

At first she said she didn't think so, because she couldn't really allow four extra people to go without opening it up to everyone, and anyway they'd have to take the other minibus and she wasn't sure if it was free. In the end, though, when we begged, she gave us a sort of exasperated smile and said, "All right, you win! Let's just check how many extra people there are going to be."

So then Izzy and I wrote her a list of all the people on the course and she phoned the other housemistresses to tell them the plan.

The next day, about fifteen extra people joined us. We all piled into the two minibuses very noisily. Miss Fosbrook, from Hazeldean, was one of the drivers and Miss Bromley, from Oakley, the other.

It wasn't till Izzy and I were sitting down with our friends that I realized I hadn't let Holly bother me at all lately. I was trying to think back to the last time she'd given me a mean look or deliberately turned her back on me, and I thought it was probably when we'd confronted her in the gym with Mrs. Truman. Had I actually seen her much since then?

"Perhaps I'm just getting used to her coldness," I said to Izzy.

"Maybe she's realized that there's no point being horrible to you because you aren't bothered!" said Bryony.

"Yes, I bet Bryony's right!" Izzy said. Then her eyes suddenly widened and she hunched her shoulders. "It's the race today! I'm so scared!"

I didn't feel at all scared, though, because I didn't mind who won. I was just a bit sad because it had suddenly sunk in that this was the last time I'd be here at Pollington Water this term.

"I'm going to ask Mum and Dad if I can go sculling for a birthday present in the holidays!" I told Izzy quietly, thinking that I wouldn't mind if I had that as a present for every birthday and every Christmas for the rest of my life.

"Good one!" she said, cheering up again.

Emily and the others absolutely loved Pollington Water the moment they set eyes on it, and Izzy and I felt proud showing them round the boathouse and explaining everything.

"Look! All the boats have names!" said Antonia. "I will find my favourite!" A moment later she announced that it was *Carla Conrad*. "Because Carla is an Italian name!"

Down on the landing stage, it felt strange having our friends there watching. Ryan said we could have twenty minutes' warm-up, then he was going to get the race under way. I'd been so sure I didn't mind who won the race, but the moment we were in that quad, I felt determination rushing through my whole body. It wasn't that I particularly wanted to beat Holly's team, just that I wanted my own team to win. I'd never been competitive about anything before, so it came as a bit of a shock.

We worked hard during the warm-up, but not too hard, because I wanted Izzy and the others to save their energy. As we were practising, George and Ben were putting buoys out to mark the course for the race. Then Ryan called us together. He said that the race would be four hundred metres in length, that Poppy's team would be setting off first, then there'd be a whistle for my team to set off, and shortly after that there'd be another whistle for Holly's team. I glanced at Holly but her face showed nothing.

When it was time to get the three boats lined up for the start I called, "Okay, we're on the start... Bow, take a stroke. Just a light one...that's enough." Sabrina had done as I said. "Come forward... and keep relaxed. We'll square up the blades in a minute."

My crew rested their blades on the water as Ryan called, "Attention team one..."

Straight away there seemed to be a new feeling in the air. Concentration. Energy.

"Go!"

And Poppy's team set off.

From that moment on, our little audience on the landing stage started cheering and I realized it had been a great idea to ask Mrs. Pridham if we could have supporters. They made a good atmosphere so the race seemed somehow more special. But, all the same, it was important to keep my team concentrating. "We're drifting a little... I need another stroke, bow... That's fine... Let's square up now," I said, as I waited for Ryan's call.

"Team two... Attention!"

"Ready, crew...?" I said, swallowing.

"Go!" came Ryan's command.

My heart thumped as I tried to keep my voice loud enough above the noise from the audience on the landing stage, but calm enough for my crew to feel confident. Poppy's team seemed to have drawn so far away. We had a lot of catching up to do, but we were getting there, and I was determined we'd do even better.

The whistle for team three to start seemed to come after no time at all, and though it was worrying in one way, I also felt quite flattered that

Ryan can't have thought Holly's crew was that much better than ours, as he didn't give us much of a start over them.

"Come on. Keep it up!" I yelled, because when I turned round I could see that Holly's team was rowing hard and gaining on us a bit already. Everyone in my team tried even harder and I realized we were really catching up with team one. It was such a wonderful moment when we pulled ahead of them! Then out towards the island we whooshed, pulling and pushing, pulling and pushing, in perfect rhythm with each other.

"Don't worry!" Ryan called to Poppy from his little dinghy nearby. "You're doing fine. Just keep going!" But a big groan came from her boat.

The next time I turned round I saw that Holly's team was gaining on us and no matter how much I kept encouraging my team, they just couldn't go any faster. They all looked exhausted. Team three overtook us only seconds before the buoy that marked the finish of the race, and a great cheer went up from their boat and from the landing stage.

"You were amazing!" said Antonia, patting me and Izzy on the back when we were on dry land once more.

"Yes, well done!" said Nicole.

"Holly's lucky, she's got all the strong rowers on her boat," said Emily, probably trying to make me feel better about coming second. But the truth was, I wasn't disappointed. My team had sculled better than ever before and I felt proud of them and told them so.

"Good work, Sasha!" Ryan called out as he walked towards us. "And well done, team two. I can't believe how much you've improved." Then, turning to me, he said, "I bet you'd like to get sculling again though, wouldn't you?"

I nodded happily. "Yes, I like coxing, but my favourite thing is definitely sculling."

"Excellent, because later I have plans for you and Holly." He beckoned her over to where we were standing. Everyone else stood round talking excitedly about the race and what fun it had been, and as the spectators spilled out their congratulations to the winners and their condolences to the losers, I followed Ryan and Holly further along the landing stage, to where Celia was crouching, holding on to a boat.

I heard myself gasp and, beside me, Holly seemed dumbstruck. It was the most beautiful, gleaming, racing scull double I'd seen yet.

"Yes," said Ryan, smiling at our shocked faces. "This is a top-class double. A proper racing scull. I want to fast-track you two because I'm so impressed with the extraordinary progress you've each made. I've actually never seen anything like it in such a short time. You've definitely gone beyond stable sculls now, so this –" his hand reached out towards the wonderful, long slim boat – "is your next challenge!"

I felt something tighten inside me at the same time as my heart sang. The thought of sculling in this amazing boat was like a dream come true. But sculling with Holly? Would the dream turn into a nightmare?

Chapter Nine

It was five thirty on Wednesday afternoon and Holly and I were arriving at Pollington Water in Miss Fosbrook's car, for our special extra session in the amazing racing double. Holly was sitting in the front beside Miss Fosbrook and I'd been left on my own in the back. It was a relief that Miss Fosbrook had been chattering away throughout the journey, because it made it less obvious that Holly and I never actually said a single word to each other, but only ever spoke to Miss Fosbrook.

As soon as we'd parked, Holly got out and rushed ahead of me to the boathouse, and by the time I got there Ben had come out and was heading off towards the lake.

"Hi, Sasha," he called. "Holly needs a hand with taking the boat down to the landing stage. Ryan's waiting for you."

When I saw the boat that Holly was standing beside, the thrill I got was just as great as when I'd seen it in the lake at the end of the last session. At least I *thought* this was the same boat. It was difficult to tell, because there were quite a few in the boathouse that looked the same.

Holly and I didn't speak to each other at all as we carried the boat down to the lakeside, where Ryan was helping some boys who looked like beginners.

"Well done," said Ryan, scarcely looking at us. He broke off what he was doing with the boys for just a few seconds to ease our boat into the water, then called out to Ben to take over with the boys so he could work with me and Holly.

"No shoes this time, girls," he began, "because there are fixed shoes attached to the bottom of the boat." As we bent down to take our trainers off, Ryan carried on talking. "There are just the two positions, bow and stroke. And there's no rudder, so it'll be up to the person at bow to be responsible for steering and telling the one at stroke where to go."

"Which position needs the stronger sculler?" asked Holly.

"They're pretty much the same," said Ryan, "but the person at bow has a bit more responsibility."

We did up the gates on the landing-stage side, then Ryan told me to get into the boat while Holly held on to it. "That's right, Sasha, you're at bow. Now do up your other gate."

Next I held on to the landing stage while Holly got in at stroke, and did up her gate.

It felt funny pushing my feet into the shoes that were attached to a metal plate, when we were used to just having a Velcro strap to stick over our own shoes in the stable sculls. I was wondering if I'd be able to get my feet out if we lost our balance and fell in, but then I'd managed all right during the capsize drill, so...

Ryan must have seen me looking anxious. "The heels have a thin stringy strap keeping them attached to the boat, so don't worry, you'll be able to whip your feet out quickly if you do happen to capsize." He gave us both a big grin. "But there's no way that's going to happen, two old hands like you two."

"Now, Sasha," he went on, "I want you just to rest your hands on the blades but don't paddle at all,

127

then you'll be acting as a stabilizer for the scull. Holly, you start to paddle gently to get the feel of how light the scull is... That's right, gently does it. Don't paddle at all with the left blade...good... Now ease round so you're lined up ready to go straight back. Sasha, turn round from time to time to check the direction, and tell Holly if she needs to pull harder on one side to steer."

I was so relieved that Ryan was staying with us, because it felt really scary to be in charge of such a fine scull. But the other reason it was good to have him close by was because I was so nervous about being on my own with Holly.

Once she'd been practising for a little time it was my turn to paddle, while she stayed perfectly still. As soon as I began, it was the best feeling I'd had since I'd first realized I could scull. This scull was altogether different from the stable ones and after this I knew I'd never want to go back to a stable one again. It's hard to explain, but I almost felt I was a part of this boat, and trying not to wobble was the best challenge in the world.

I had a good long go and then we each had one more shorter turn before Ryan said we were ready to start working as a team. We had to use just our arms at first and then gradually increase the stroke length until we were using our legs as well and taking really long strokes. I thought how brilliant it would be if we really could work as a team. It would be just so cool if Holly and I got on well with each other and trained together, and I could think of her as my sculling partner. But there was no way that would ever happen.

"Looking good," said Ryan, grinning. Then he called to George, who was in another boat not far off. "Pretty good pair, eh?"

George gave us a thumbs up and called out that we looked really professional, which was a lovely compliment. Soon I could feel that Holly was speeding up, yet I was sure I remembered Ryan saying that, although Holly should set the rhythm, she shouldn't speed up unless I asked her to. Maybe she was irritated with me for not wanting to go fast enough. I pushed on my legs a bit harder to match her speed and we really seemed to put a spurt on.

"That's great!" called Ryan. "Go as far as you want but not right round the island, because I want to keep you in sight. I won't be far away, but if you carry on like you are at the moment, you'll be back in no time!"

Neither Holly nor I said a word, and yet, in a funny way, we *were* a good team, because somehow we were managing to keep in time instinctively. Although Holly was setting the pace, I was fitting in completely naturally.

In the end I was so happy with the way we were managing that I just had to say something. After all there was no one else anywhere near us – it was just us and the scull and the cold blue water – so it felt a bit odd that we were both completely silent. "Good, isn't it?" was all I could think of saying.

There was a pause and I felt my stomach tightening, because it didn't seem like she was going to reply. But then she did. "Uh-huh."

That was all she said. It was better than nothing, though.

Up till then we'd been going more or less in a straight line, but we had to turn slightly now, which meant that I had to tell Holly what to do. I swallowed.

"Right oar lighter, Holly," I managed, a bit shakily.

She did as I said, and did it again when I asked her to do the same thing a few moments later. So then we sculled through a lovely stretch of water that we'd never tried before. And that was when I was suddenly aware that Holly was pulling harder again, getting us to go faster. Apart from telling her to slow down, which I didn't want to do, there was nothing for it except to try to keep up with the speed she was setting. But my legs were beginning to ache. Still, she was probably right to stretch us. Ryan would surely approve if he was watching.

For three or four minutes I managed to keep up with her, but when she pulled even harder I thought my lungs were going to burst and I didn't know how Holly was managing. I'd never realized she was such a strong sculler. No wonder she'd been impatient with me for not asking her to go faster. She was way better than me. I pushed as hard as I possibly could and was on the point of telling her that she'd have to slow down because I couldn't keep up, when the scull suddenly juddered and I realized that something was very wrong.

Holly's arms must have given out, because one of her blades slapped the water at completely the wrong angle and she lost her grip on the other. The scull was wobbling.

"Try to keep hold of the blades, Holly," I said, fearing the worst and thinking back desperately to what we'd been taught in the capsize drill.

I concentrated hard on staying as still as I possibly could, because that was the only way we were going to stop the scull from capsizing. But Holly was flailing about and saying, "Oh no! Oh no!"

"It's okay, Holly, try not to panic, we'll be okay…"

But the boat was lurching further and further down to one side.

"No, it's no good! No! No!" screamed Holly.

And that was when I knew there was nothing more I could do. I tried so hard not to panic myself, just quickly pulled my feet out of the shoes as the boat turned right over and the cold water hit me and took my breath away. I pushed myself to the surface urgently and got a terrible shock when I realized that Holly was still underneath. Then I understood with a jolt that she must have got her foot stuck in one of the shoes, so I grabbed hold of her under her arms and eased her up to get her head out of the water.

"It's okay," I said, through my chattering teeth, as I trod water hard. "I can release your foot. Just give me a second." I reached under the scull until my hand came into contact with the metal and then the shoe. I noticed at that moment that Holly's face was really white, and knew I had to work quickly. "Hold tight to the side of the scull, Holly," I said gently, as I released her foot. "There you are."

She was shivering terribly, looking really upset, and I noticed that she'd cut her arm on something.

Blood was mixing with the water, sending pink streams trickling down her arm.

"I think Ryan's spotted us. He's on his way," I carried on, trying to reassure her. And thinking about Ryan made me remember something else we'd talked about in the swimming pool when we'd done the capsize drill. "Let's leave the boat upside down, Holly. Here, I'll help you get up on top of it, then your body won't lose its heat so fast."

So that's how we waited for Ryan, me treading water, stiff and tense, Holly like a rag doll; both of us silent, both staring straight ahead. And it was only then that I noticed the name of our boat for the first time as I read it slowly upside down: *Carla Conrad*. What a coincidence! It was the name of the boat that Antonia had said she liked best.

My gaze shifted back to Holly. Her eyes were very red, and I wondered if it was because of the water or whether she'd been crying.

"Look, Ryan's just about here," I said, to try and comfort her, because I'd never seen her like this before.

"You're all right, Holly," said Ryan in a calm voice as he pulled alongside. "Come on, let's get you in here." He helped her into his little launch and wrapped her in a thermal blanket. "Don't worry about your arm. A little blood goes a long way when it's mixed with water!"

"My f-foot got stuck," Holly said in a small voice.

Ryan looked puzzled as he reached underneath our upturned scull. "Let's see," he said. "Yes," he said slowly. "That's odd. The string's broken." He looked from one to the other of us. "Did you get the boat that Ben told you to get?"

Holly didn't answer, and I didn't actually know the answer because I hadn't been there.

"Well, not to worry," Ryan carried straight on, looking at Holly's white face. "These things happen. Sit down there, Holly. That's right, it's warmer on the floor of the boat. You won't feel the wind so much." Next he turned his attention to me. "What about you, Sasha? Do you want to come in here and get warm? I can get one of the others to bring the scull back. But I reckon you'd be able to scull the double back on your own. It's up to you."

"I'll scull it back," I said firmly, even though I was shivering with cold by then.

I was determined to manage on my own and I listened carefully as Ryan gave me instructions to arrange the blades so they were parallel with the boat.

"Well done," he said. "Now stand on the rigger so you can reach the far rigger."

I did as I was told and managed to pull the boat over without getting hit by either of the blades.

"Good work!" said Ryan. "Okay, I'll hold the boat steady while you get yourself back in."

It only took me a few seconds and Ryan seemed pleased with me, but then in a more serious voice he said, "So, what exactly happened out there, girls? What do you think it was that made you capsize?"

I felt myself tensing right up, and didn't know what to say. Holly was looking down, saying nothing at all, and the silence was going on too long. Ryan, meanwhile, looked from one to the other of us, waiting.

"Er...I think it was that we both suddenly felt tired," I managed to stutter, "and kind of...lost our rhythm..."

Holly lifted up her head and turned to look at me. I wasn't sure what the look was saying, but it only lasted for a second, then her eyes went down again as Ryan began a bit of a teachery lecture, which seemed to be aimed at me. I couldn't work out why at first, but then I realized that, of course, Ryan thought *I'd* been the one to set the fast speed, because I was the one at bow.

"Well you were certainly sculling at a heck of a speed. I reckon you were just pushing yourselves too hard." He leaned forward a little and looked straight into my eyes. "Try not to be too ambitious next time, please?"

I felt myself going red, even though I knew I hadn't done anything wrong, and that made me cross with myself. Why didn't I just tell Ryan what had really happened? But I knew the answer to that question. I was scared of how Holly would react.

"Right." Ryan nodded, as if to signal that the inquisition was over. Then he got on his phone and started talking to one of the coaches at the landing stage to ask her to get towels organized and a warm drink, and also to ask Miss Fosbrook to fetch Holly's and my dry clothes from her car. He then asked for another coach to come out and check I got in safely.

"Celia's on her way. You'll be fine now, Sasha," he said, turning to me as he put his mobile back in his pocket.

I nodded.

"Okay, see you back there!"

Then he was gone. But as he switched on the motor and his launch zoomed off I saw that Holly had sat up and was looking at me. Our eyes met just for a second and there seemed to be a question in them, but I didn't know what it was.

I got a nice surprise when I found myself back on dry land, because the coaches and various other students I'd never met before were acting as though I was a hero, congratulating me on looking after Holly and then managing to get the boat back in. Two students who were quite a bit older than me said they'd walked round the lake and seen us from another angle and thought how professional we looked. Miss Fosbrook laughed and said she'd give me a big hug once I was dry, but she didn't want to get sopping wet herself. Then she told me she thought Holly and I were amazing rowers, and one little capsize didn't matter. I thought how kind she was being.

Celia gave me a hot drink and told me to take it up to the clubhouse, where Holly was getting changed and where Miss Fosbrook had left my dry clothes. I made my way up there, feeling my footsteps dragging as I drew nearer, because I so didn't want to find myself alone with Holly again.

"Hi," she said as I went in, which gave me a shock, because I'd been expecting her usual silence.

But then I got an even bigger shock, because she was giving me a sort of wobbly smile.

I grabbed my clothes and took them into the loo to get changed in private, as it was easier than being with Holly. But when I came out I found she was still standing there in exactly the same position she'd been in before, and was staring at me with round eyes in her pale face.

"I...did something I shouldn't have done..." she said hesitantly.

I waited, wondering what on earth she was going to say.

"I...I didn't take the boat Ben told me to take."

My head was spinning, because at that moment I thought I understood what must have happened, and yet...I couldn't believe it.

"I didn't think it mattered. The one I took looked just the same...only I liked the name better."

I could tell from her eyes there was more to come, so I waited, my heart beating with the gradual realization that my guess had been right.

"Ryan was really cross with me just now. He said the boat I took was waiting to have the heel restraint changed. That's why...my foot got stuck."

I nodded but stayed silent, feeling suddenly sorry for her as she looked so upset.

"Th-thank you for not telling Ryan it was my fault that we capsized," she then said, in the same small voice she'd used in the boat.

And suddenly I understood what the question in her eyes had been. She'd wanted to know why I hadn't told Ryan the real reason we'd capsized.

I didn't know what to say. "Er...that's...okay."

Holly's voice still sounded weak. "He knows... now, because...I've told him what happened... really."

I still wasn't sure what to say, and when I thought about it, I didn't actually know what had happened myself. "So...what *did* happen, Holly?" I asked her quietly.

She drew her breath in slowly, then began to speak hesitantly. "I thought...you might be wishing...we could go faster. I thought you...might be bored rowing with me. When Ryan put you at bow I worried that he didn't think I was as good as you...and..." Suddenly she started gabbling at full speed and the words tumbled out of her mouth as her eyes grew bigger and bigger, which made her face seem paler and paler. "I felt stupid because I've done lots of sculling before and you hadn't done any, and yet you were just as good as me... And I had to prove myself. So I just kept talking to myself, telling myself to try harder…but you were easily keeping up, so then I tried to make myself go even faster, and still you were easily keeping up—"

I had to interrupt her because she'd got that so wrong. "No, I wasn't. My arms were dropping off!"

"So were mine!" she said.

And then she stopped and looked at me, and I saw her eyes change, and that made mine change too, because I wondered if she was picturing us, like I was, in our double scull out there on the lake, both struggling away, because we each thought the other wanted to go faster. And the picture was so funny that I suddenly burst out laughing and a second later so did Holly.

It was one of those giggling fits that almost hurts your stomach, because you're laughing so hard, and I knew Holly felt the same, because she clutched her stomach with one hand and reached out to lean on me with the other. And there we stood, doubled over, laughing our heads off, until Holly's arm went round my shoulder and she suddenly hugged me and whispered, "Sorry, Sasha."

"That's okay," I said, feeling my throat hurting, because there was something really touching about those two words of hers. I knew it must have taken a lot for her to say them.

She drew back but kept her eyes on mine. "No, I mean sorry for…everything. I was just so…jealous. You see, I've always been pretty average at sports and I was so happy when I heard that we could do this sculling course, because I could show people that at least I was good at something, but then I felt as though you were better than me and kind of taking over."

"I didn't mean to…"

"I know you didn't. It was totally my fault."

"But thank you for not telling on me about using the rowing machine that time when there were no teachers around," I said, feeling my face getting hot.

"Well, actually…to tell the truth, I'd already had a go on it myself!"

I gasped and was about to jokingly tell her off when I saw that her eyes had filled with tears. So then it was me hugging *her*. And that's how we were when Celia came in.

"Aha!" said Celia, her eyes dancing. "Sign of a true teamship. Big hugs after an accident!" Then she laughed at herself. "Not sure if there's such a word as a 'teamship', but I quite like it anyway!"

Holly and I both laughed happily, then Ryan appeared.

"Do you want the bad news or the good news?" he asked.

Neither Holly nor I spoke.

"Okay, well the bad news," he said, plunging on, "is that the course is well and truly finished, even for you two."

I nodded, feeling a weight of sadness come over me.

"But the good news is that there's an inter-school double sculls race next Wednesday at five o'clock. It's a very highly regarded race and we've got someone famous presenting the trophy to the winning team. Three schools have entered, and as you two have proved yourselves to be exceptional, I've already got permission from Silver Spires for you to be in it too! No one's expecting you to win, obviously, but it'll be great experience. So now there are four schools!"

I felt a gasp of pure happiness welling up inside me as I turned to Holly and saw that her tears seemed to be sparkling now.

"That's so cool!" she said, reaching for my hand.

Ryan looked at me.

"Yes, it's fantastic," I agreed, gripping Holly's hand tight, "because we're such a good teamship!"

Chapter Ten

The four double sculls were lined up side by side. Holly and I were in lane three. We were both watching the landing stage to see if my dad had arrived, because the race wasn't due to start for another few minutes. Holly had already spotted her parents.

"You said he'd be wearing a suit, didn't you?" she said, scouring the lakeside, where loads of people were standing around, including all my friends.

Emily kept jumping up and down doing two-handed waves but there was no way I could wave back like that or I might tip the scull over. Antonia was on one side of her and Izzy on the other and they seemed to be taking turns to try and hold her arms down. I guess Izzy realized it would be awful if I waved back by mistake and then fell in.

Bryony was taking lots of photos and Nicole was talking to someone standing nearby. But there was still no sign of my dad.

I'd been so happy when I'd phoned home and told Mum all about what had happened with Holly and the double scull. As usual, though, after a minute or two she'd sounded as though she wasn't concentrating and had put Dad on the phone.

"Well, that's brilliant, Sash!" he'd said, sounding really proud of me. "We'll definitely have to sort you out some sculling in the holidays." Then he said he'd been talking to a friend of his who knew of a really good sculling club about forty-five minutes away from where we live. "We'll get you booked in there, and you can scull to your heart's content!"

After that I'd told him about the race that we'd be competing in.

"It's eight hundred metres, dad. That's twice as long as our other race!"

Dad seemed really impressed and pleased for me, but didn't offer to come along. I actually thought it was silly of me to expect it. I hadn't even thought of it until Holly told me she'd invited her parents and they were coming. But mine live much further away and they had the twins to think about too, so I knew really that there was no way they could come. In the end, though, I asked Dad. Just in case.

"Wednesday at five?" he said. And I could hear paper rustling and guessed he was looking through his diary. I got myself ready to be disappointed, but then the best thing happened because he said, "You know what, I've got a meeting only about an hour away from Silver Spires on that day, so I reckon I could make it by five if I got a move on. Tell you what," he added, "I'll bring my DVD camera, then Mum can see it when I get back!"

"Oh Dad! That would be great!" I said.

And now the race was about to start, but I still couldn't see him.

"Never mind," said Holly, trying to cheer me up. "Remember Ryan said there's someone famous presenting the trophy? I wonder if they're here."

I certainly did remember, and I'd been wondering all day who it might be. "I can't see anyone famous out there, can you?" I asked Holly.

"There's a man there talking to my parents," said Holly. Then she laughed. "I don't mean a famous man! Just that it might be your dad!"

I looked across to where I knew Holly's parents were standing, but it wasn't Dad talking to them and my heart lurched with disappointment. What if Dad didn't make it in time? What if he'd got held up in traffic?

"And now there's a man and a woman talking to Izzy..." said Holly.

My eyes shifted back to where Izzy was standing with the others and my heart missed a beat because there was Dad and *Mum*!

"They've both come!" I said to Holly. "I can't believe it. My mum's come too! She must have left the twins with Grandma and Grandpa!"

"Hey, that's brilliant, Sash!" said Holly warmly. "We've both got our parents here. Let's make them proud!"

Just as she said that, an official-sounding voice came over the loudspeaker, announcing that the race was about to start, and I felt myself tensing up. He named all the schools competing and my heart beat faster when I heard him mention Silver Spires School for Girls.

"Here goes!" said Holly quietly.

"Here goes!" I echoed.

"Attention!" came the voice over the loudspeaker. This was it. "...Go!"

Somewhere in the distance there seemed to be a lot of shouting and cheering, but all I could really hear was the sound of our blades swishing against the water, and our breathing, exactly in time with each other. I gave my instructions to Holly in a much quieter voice than before, because we were such a team now, totally working together and tuned into each other. As we rounded the first slight bend in the course there was only one boat ahead of us. I'd seen these girls getting into their scull and thought at the time how much bigger they looked than Holly and me, and now they were proving that they were stronger too.

I knew I should have been focusing one hundred per cent on rowing at that moment, but I couldn't help the thought of Mum watching me, cutting into my concentration. I so wanted her to be proud of me.

"We can do it," I said through clenched teeth to Holly.

"Yes, we can," she replied.

And I didn't have to say anything else, we both just pulled and pushed together, our breathing getting louder as our bodies reached forward and pulled back, reached forward and pulled back. We'd done a massive semicircle round the island and I could see the yew tree with its bright yellow marker way up ahead of us. We had to keep in line with that marker and scull between two yellow buoys, which denoted the finishing line. Whichever boat passed that line first, would win the race.

It was so tempting to keep going fast with short strokes but I knew we'd tire ourselves out. I spoke as firmly as I could, my breath coming in bursts. "Okay, long and strong…relax and drive."

Holly did exactly what I'd said and a few moments later, when I turned to check our direction, I knew it was our last chance to put on a final spurt if we possibly had the energy for it, because the scull ahead of us was really close to the finishing line.

I turned one last time to check we were in line with the marker, and realized at the same time that the spectators on the lakeside had all moved round to the yew tree so they could see the sculls coming in to the finish. They were already starting to shout out but I couldn't hear what they were saying.

"Okay, drive!" I yelled.

And we did just that, straining every sinew in our bodies to make our scull cut its way through the water, catching up with the other boat until we found ourselves level with them.

"Drive now! Legs now!" I screeched. And with one final push we passed them. And the crowd on the lakeside yelled even more loudly.

"The winners!" came Ryan's voice over the loudhailer. "By half a length! Sasha Turner and Holly Johns for Silver Spires!"

And my heart sang with triumph.

"In second place, Becky Goodwin and Tara Steele for Whitington College."

"We did it!" whispered Holly, as we paddled gently round to the landing stage, sweating and red, puffing and panting, but so, so happy. Celia and Ben helped us out of the sculls, and it was a good job they did, because our legs and arms were trembling too much to manage on our own.

"I feel like a rag doll!" said Holly, as she gave me a hug. Then we both flopped down, totally exhausted and unable to speak, yet unable to stop grinning at each other triumphantly. I thought back to the last time Holly had reminded me of a rag doll. Things were so different now. So very different. We'd both proved ourselves. And we'd done it together. I couldn't have been happier.

Well, that's what I thought at that moment. But then I saw Mum rushing through the crowd, her arms outstretched.

"Oh, Sash!" she said. And as she came right up to me I saw that there were tears in her eyes. "You were so brilliant! I can't believe it! I'm so proud of you!" Then she wrapped her arms round me and I felt, just then, as though I was snuggled right into the centre of her world.

"Totally fantastic!" said Dad, appearing a second later. "I don't know how ever you managed that last stretch."

Mum let me go of me so Dad could give me a hug, and I saw that Holly was getting hugs and cuddles from her parents too. Then Izzy and the others appeared. They were hanging back a bit, so I went and grabbed Izzy's hand and the others followed. After that, it was just completely mad with everyone congratulating us. And I didn't have to do anything except enjoy it.

Once the other two boats were in and Ryan had gathered everyone round, he stood at the front of the crowd with a small lady, who I guessed was probably in her thirties.

"That must be the famous person," Izzy whispered to me.

I nodded, wondering who she was.

"Oh my goodness!" Mum said under her breath. "How brilliant!"

So Mum recognized her. Who could she be? I couldn't ask because Ryan had picked up the loudspeaker to make his announcement.

"It is with the greatest of pleasure that I introduce you all to former Olympic gold medallist, Carla Conrad!"

There was a burst of applause from the crowd while Holly and I stared at each other, dumbfounded, then broke into smiles at exactly the same moment. "I knew there was a reason why I liked that boat so much!" whispered Holly, her eyes twinkling. A splutter of laughter rose up inside me.

"Carla actually trained here at the Pollington Water Club as a girl, and one of the boats is named after her, so please give her an especially warm welcome."

When the cheering and clapping had died down, Carla began to speak.

"It's wonderful to be back here after so many years," she began, "and to find the club almost unchanged. I watched the race just now and was transported right back to my childhood. Such wonderful, strong and happy memories, of being eleven years old, like many of you here today, when

I first realized that I had a gift for sculling. I will never forget the magic of that moment. So now it is with great pleasure that I present this fine-boat trophy –" she held up a shiny gold model double scull – "to Sasha Turner and Holly Johns of Silver Spires School, the winners of today's race!"

As loud applause broke out, Holly led the way forward to collect the golden trophy.

"Excellent work, Holly," Carla said. "You are a very worthy winner indeed!"

Then Holly moved to one side, and when I shook Carla's hand she looked right into my eyes and spoke very quietly so no one else would have been able to hear her. Not even Holly.

"I see a great future for you, Sasha, and I will be listening out for your name in the Olympic village."

I felt close to tears of happiness as Holly and I walked away, holding the beautiful model of a golden scull between us. I felt as though we were in our own little world, because all around us the clapping and cheering was louder than ever, and Ryan was whooping through the loudspeaker.

"You deserve this more than I do," Holly said quietly, handing it to me.

"No, it's equal. It's to share," I told her.

"Please take it," she said.

"Well only for a minute. So I can show Mum and Dad and my friends."

I smiled my head off as I walked over to them, then, "It's beautiful!" said Antonia. "And see, it says *Carla Conrad* on the side here!"

"What did she say to you?" Izzy asked me quietly.

"She said she'd be listening out for my name..." I couldn't say the next bit. It sounded too show-offy. "...Because she thinks I have a great future. Isn't that lovely?"

"Well you do have a great future!" said Izzy. "Sasha the super sculler!"

And I looked round my smiling friends – Emily the eco warrior, Bryony the brave one, Nicole the brainy one, Antonia the international one and Izzy the dancer. It was so brilliant that I'd found my place amongst them.

Sasha the super sculler.

I liked that.

Sasha's Top Team-building Exercises

Teamwork is the key to success, not just when it comes to sculling, but in many other activities such as drama, orchestra, choir and sports. Here are my top three team-building exercises, guaranteed to get you giggling, help you make new friends and turn you into team players!

Guess Who?

Pick a "guesser" from your group and ask them to leave the room. Now pick your leader, who starts doing an action on the spot for the whole group to copy. The leader can change the action to a different one whenever they like. When the guesser enters they must try and spot the leader by working out who's setting off each new action. If you're in the group, try not to look at the leader...
it's more fun, and trickier too!

Bump in the Night

Set up a safe obstacle course using pillows, chairs, boxes, beanbags or whatever you have to hand. Now blindfold a member of your group and spin them around gently. Now direct your blindfolded player through the course as a team, without touching them. Only one person may direct at any time, but everyone must give directions at some point in the game. If your player bumps into anything, or you talk over each other in the team,

then it's back to the start!

Pat on the Back

Tape a piece of paper to everyone's back and then give everyone a washable marker pen. Move around the group so that each person writes one nice thing on one other person's back. Then get your team leader to collect all the papers and read out the compliments. Can you guess which one was for you?

Trust me; it's an unbeatable morale booster.

So what are you waiting for? Get out there and have some fun!

Sasha

Now read on for a sneak preview of

Mystery at Silver Spires

It was the middle of the night. I mean, the *very* middle of the night. Our dormitory was pitch black.

"Bryony, are you awake?" Izzy's trembling whisper came out of the darkness.

"Yes," I whispered back.

"Did you hear that noise?"

"I'm not sure...*something* must have woken me up..." I switched on my little night light. Then I looked round the other four beds in the dorm, but the rest of our friends were still fast asleep.

After a moment, when my eyes had adjusted

properly, I could see Izzy's pale frightened face. "Don't worry, Izzy. It's probably just one of those creaks you sometimes get in old buildings." But even as I was talking, I was thinking, *What rubbish*, because our boarding house, Forest Ash, is only about forty years old. I mean, that's not exactly ancient.

"Where do you think the noise came from?" Izzy whispered. "I couldn't tell."

I was about to say I wasn't sure when it came again – a soft bump. Izzy looked terrified and, though my heart was beating faster than usual, I felt sure there had to be an obvious explanation. "It could be a mouse or a bird," I said, trying not to sound too anxious. "After all we're on the top floor here. There's only the attic above us and nobody ever goes up there. I wouldn't even know how to get to it."

"But it didn't sound like a scratchy, scrabbly noise, did it, Bry?"

To find out what happens next, read

Mystery at Silver Spires

Complete your

School Friends

collection!

First Term at Silver Spires   ISBN 9780746072240
Katy's nervous about going to boarding school for the first time – especially with the big secret she has to hide.

Drama at Silver Spires   ISBN 9780746072257
Georgie's desperate to get her favourite part in the school play, but she's up against some stiff competition.

Rivalry at Silver Spires   ISBN 9780746072264
Grace is eager to win in the swimming gala for Hazeldean – until someone starts sending mean messages about her.

Princess at Silver Spires   ISBN 9780746089576
Naomi hates being the centre of attention, but when she's asked to model for a charity fashion show, she can't say no.

Secrets at Silver Spires   ISBN 9780746089583
Jess is struggling with her schoolwork and has to have special classes, but she can't bear to tell her friends the truth.

Star of Silver Spires   ISBN 9780746089590
Mia longs to enter a song she's written in the Silver Spires Star contest, but she's far too scared to perform onstage.

Party at Silver Spires   ISBN 9780746098646
Nicole's determined to keep her scholarship a secret, in case it stops her from making friends with her dorm.

Dancer at Silver Spires   ISBN 9780746098653
Izzy's trying to put her hopes of becoming a ballerina behind her – until the school puts on a dance show.

Dreams at Silver Spires   ISBN 9780746098660
Emily dreams of starting a cool club at school...but first she must persuade the teachers she's got what it takes.

Magic at Silver Spires   ISBN 9780746098677
Antonia and her friends must prove to her parents that she belongs at Silver Spires...before they take her back to Italy!

Success at Silver Spires   ISBN 9780746098684
Sasha is delighted when she discovers her natural talent for sports, but she faces tough competition from a rival.

Mystery at Silver Spires   ISBN 9780746098691
Bryony keeps hearing spooky noises in the night. Is the school haunted, or has the dorm got an unexpected guest?

Want to know more about the
Silver Spires girls?

Or try a quiz to discover which
School Friend you're most like?

You can even send Silver Spires e-cards
to your best friends and post your own
book reviews online!

It's all at

www.silverspiresschool.co.uk

 Check it out now!

For more fun and friendship-packed reads
go to **www.fiction.usborne.com**